A
SOLDIER'S
BOOK

This Large Print Book carries the
Seal of Approval of N.A.V.H.

A
SOLDIER'S
BOOK

Joanna Higgins

Thorndike Press • Thorndike, Maine

Published in 1998 by arrangement with The Permanent Press.

Thorndike Large Print® Americana Series.

The tree indicium is a trademark of Thorndike Press.

The text of this Large Print edition is unabridged.
Other aspects of the book may vary from the original edition.

Set in 16 pt. Plantin by Al Chase.

Printed in the United States on permanent paper.

Library of Congress Cataloging in Publication Data

Higgins, Joanna, 1945–
    A soldier's book / by Joanna Higgins.
        p.   cm.
    ISBN 0-7862-1594-1   (lg. print : hc : alk. paper)
    1. United States — History — Civil War, 1861–1865 —
Prisoners and prisons — Fiction. 2. Large type books.
I. Title.
[PS3558.I3574S67   1998b]
813'.54—dc21   98-28872

For Jerry and Virginia

Foreword

At the start of the American Civil War, there was no clear policy regarding the exchange of prisoners. Initially, people in the North wanted to hang captured Confederate soldiers as "insurrectionists." They might have done so, had not the Confederate government threatened to do the same with captured Northern soldiers. With no overall policy in place, generals had to work out their own exchanges in the field. This continued until July, 1862, when both sides finally reached an agreement or "cartel."

Under the terms of the cartel, prisoners were to be held for ten days after capture, and those who could not be exchanged were to be paroled after pledging not to take up arms. This agreement remained in place until July of 1863, but the North and the South paid less and less attention to it as the war dragged on and animosity between both sides increased.

Ironically, President Lincoln's Emancipation Proclamation on January 14, 1863, did much to undermine the cartel. In reponse to the Proclamation, President Davis announced that all captured Negro soldiers

7

would be regarded as slaves and treated as such, and all commissioned officers taken in those states affected by the Proclamation were to be handed over to state authorities and punished as "criminals engaged in exciting servile insurrection."

Lincoln, in turn, declared that a Confederate soldier would be killed for every Union prisoner executed by the Confederacy. And for every Negro soldier placed in servitude, a Confederate soldier would be sent to hard labor in public works projects. This stopped the Confederacy from outright executions although it still refused to exchange Negro soldiers.

After the battles of Vicksburg and Gettysburg in 1863, Grant, in the west, and Lee in Pennsylvania, set up their own exchanges out of necessity. But these were the exceptions. On the whole, any orderly exchange of prisoners had broken down. The United States government was, by now, refusing "to exchange white for white" because Confederate soldiers were being pressed into service after their release, whereas exchanged United States prisoners had thirty or sixty-day furloughs coming and were often close to the end of their terms anyway. This halting of exchanges worked a terrible effect on the prison camps, but by this time there was so much antagonism between the two sides that any remedy seemed impossible.

When Grant became Lieutenant General in command of all Union armies in 1864, he took the expedient course, at the beginning of the spring campaign, of stopping all prisoner exchanges. But by the end of that year, General Grant, affected by reports of the horrendous conditions in the camps and realizing that the Confederacy could not sustain itself much longer, argued for a return to the original cartel and "man-for-man" exchanges.

A Soldier's Book opens, however, in the spring of 1864, when all exchanges had been halted. Being captured and put into one of the increasingly overcrowded prison camps at that unfortunate time was often tantamount to a death sentence.

Source: *Harper's Pictorial History of The Civil War*, by Alfred H. Guernsey and Henry M. Alden, (New York: The Fairfax Press, 1866, reproduced and distributed by Crown Publishers Inc., New York), pp. 792-797.

There are events that will daily occur in the camp, on the field, or in the hospital, which will be interesting to every soldier, if spared, hereafter to review; and if he fall, they will be doubly interesting to his friends, could they be known . . . With this book and a lead-pencil in pocket or haversack, such a record can easily be made . . . and then, some of these Diaries, with their brief records even, may be important hereafter, in furnishing materials for History . . .

Preface, *Soldier's Diary and Book for Leisure Moments*

No returns have been rendered of the separate losses during the seven days, from May 5 to 11. The entire number is given together as follows: killed 3288; wounded, 19,278; missing 6844; total, 29,410. Allowing, as we have done, 20,000 for the Wilderness, there remains fully 10,000 for these three days at Spottsylvania. The Confederate loss is wholly a matter of estimate. In placing it at 15,000 during this period, we can not very greatly err.

— Ulysses S. Grant, Lieutenant-General

One

This cattle car a stench but at least a quiet one. For now. No moaning, fussing or cussing. Every sweet its sour, every sour its sweet. We're rocking southward, farther and deeper downward into the valley of darkness. When I close my eyes I see everything I do not want to see. When I keep my eyes open, I see more of the same. I think of provoking some argument with one of the guards. I mull the possibility of jumping and then they will have to shoot me. Why I don't do either of these things I don't know.

I believe I do. I have made so many wrong decisions that I fear making any decision now whatsoever, knowing it can only be the wrong one. So I sit here in this sour mess of a cattle car, eyeing the fouled water barrel but not even able to get myself up and go there. I am a gone-up case, as they say. I am pot and kettle overboard. From the looks of us, I'd say we all are. Guards, too. It is raining. South Carolina all rolling fog. Looks ashy as if everything is burning away. The flies in this car are laying low. The guards sit with drooping heads. I really should run.

That's what I'm thinking as the car jostles

and creaks, but it's a far-away thought, as if somebody else is thinking it and I am only hearing the echo.

This is day thirteen of our captivity. Early on, we thought our boys might stumble on the bunch of us being marched, by night, to Gordonsville, in Virginia. There'd be a skirmish and we'd run. You could almost hear everybody thinking this. Hope is an odd thing.

Thirteen days. That's near two weeks. Two weeks has reduced us from being soldiers in the Army of the Potomac into commodities, each body of us worth one reb soldier in trade. About twice the worth of a bushel of oats or wheat.

So they're keeping us alive, more or less, sometimes robbing themselves to do it. But you can see there's sure no love in it. In Gordonsville, Virginia, they relieved us of all greenbacks, rations, ammunition and arms, haversacks and cartridge boxes and cap boxes, cross belts, waist belts, canteens, as well as my compass and change of clothing. Why they did not take our coats and blankets I do not know. Gus says it's because we ain't cavalry. They hate cavalry beyond all else and will rob them of everything but their pants.

I have my *Soldier's Book for Leisure Moments* and my father's pen, and a Brazil silver spoon found on the Gordonsville Road. Also some thread and a needle. If I run, I will put these items near Gus so when he wakes up, there they'll be. He lost all his bounty pay to them.

I find that if I pay attention to things right now, it's better. Gus taught me this. Right now I'm looking at him. He is a small and trim man, with white hair curving away from his forehead but his beard and moustache still fairly dark. You wouldn't believe he's asleep, the way he's sitting up so straight. Veterans know how to do that. He is going to wind up the most rested captive in all of Georgia.

For that's where we're going, is the new rumor.

My own eyes feel rubbed in sand.

It's warmer now the rain's stopped. Flies again.

The worse-handled a guard has been, the easier they are on us. A person might think just the opposite, but no. These in this car look like they have been through three wars. No uniforms, shirts with a year's worth of tobacco juice painted on 'em, boots looped up with twine. One man has a black patch like a pirate and squints with his other eye, as if holding us up to the light. Probably can't see worth half a bean. I should run.

Know why I don't. Gus. He'd probably come after me again and get shot. I'd be the one not to.

Hardly a one of us believes this fortunate turn. Bathing in a stream while awaiting a transfer at some station. We have eaten good corn pone and drunk our bellies full of clean water. Georgia, our new guards are saying. Ain't no scrimpers here, like some places, they said, serving up that corn pone. In good humor, maybe to be home. All around, piney hillsides rise up sharp. Everything ascends. The light, too, sparking off these deep pools. Everywhere I look is green. But this ain't no place to run.

Reminds me of the Wilderness, which I don't care to remember but do. The way we marched straight into those woods all brambles and bunched-together trees, and stumps bristly with sucker grown, and stone outcroppings, and piles of grown-over brush, and ravines with steep inclines and stony creeks at the bottom, all that mess breaking apart our ranks in no time. And we foolish enough to think that whatever rebs might be

14

around were in fast retreat before our so-called advance. Flowers along the creeks, the nicest little flowers. Closing my eyes now, I can see them. Yellow. Six petals. Gold, furry centers. Can see a bird lifting up out of a tree as viney on top as at the bottom. Can hear the first shots up ahead, see the woods go gray with powder charge, see myself running, blackberry canes snagging and ripping at my uniform, and then I'm firing my ramrod into a pine, exactly like they told us not to, then running some more, forgetting to get the ramrod, running because I am twisted around and lost, then coming to a glade and being so happy to see Federal blue, but then stopping like a shot man — at the flies, the blood seeping into that blue, our boys strewn about like blown laundry in them brambles, and one of the dying boys saying, Son, some water — But I run like something crazed until Gus intercepts me, Gus come searching for me.

Open my eyes and find I am afloat in a stream musical as any. And sun pouring down. No fire coming. No dead and dying boys thrown about in brambles. But in the stream-music I hear it, that wall of fire, and I see myself running, loaded down as a jack mule and clattering like some broken down engine.

I try to think of the minute under my nose.

Hear a furling that is only water.

See a stretch of blue sky, a river up there too, glowing between the hilltops.

A guard hollers something and it sounds just like the yell of those Outcasts in the Wilderness, as Gus called them, who captured us that day, then rushed us down trails only they could fathom out.

I flop over in the water. Float like a dead man.

Day fourteen. At some lean-to siding, waiting for something. Everybody in this car hoping for some more corn pone. Each rattle from outside and we look at one another, wondering if. But it's taking too long so I've given up. When a thing's complicated it usually means it won't work out. The thing that's meant to be happens like water rushing downhill.

There's grumbling about the fragrance in here, guards grumbling too, but what can we do about it?

We have made two friends. A big fellow named Louie Val and a boy named Willy Winston. Sixteen, maybe even younger (says eighteen). Louie Val looks like a farrier. Big and rounded. Wide-set eyes. Hair black and thick and filling up his head and face, wrapping down around it and sweeping up over the top lip. Looks like black moss overtaking a stump. Willy is skinny but with a little boy's plumped up face yet. Hair so red it makes his skin pink. Jug ears. A sharp, shrewd look most of the time.

They were caught in the Wilderness too, but asleep on their arms. Louie keeps telling this story over and over. How they were on alert for thirty-six hours, then had to have a little sleep, so an order was given to withdraw and they did and then Longstreet with his twenty thousand or so boys picks that time to show up. They got the whole regiment, Louie says, thousands of them, just like that. He always slams one hand against the other at this point. If only we didn't have to smash into each other in that damned jungle! he keeps saying. I would not like to be on his bad side. Willy is a runaway from an orphans' home in Reading. Says the grub there was terrible. Believes they put ashes and what-not in the porridge to make it stretch. Couldn't be worse in the army, he figured, so here he is now.

My book the only thing that helps me fall asleep. So I read for awhile. *A gentle breeze moves four miles an hour, a fresh breeze twelve miles, a brisk wind twenty-five miles, a very high wind sixty miles, a violent gale one hundred miles, and hurricanes still more rapidly, up to three hundred miles an hour.*

Eyes are nearly shutting nice, but Willy wants to know what I'm reading. So I read it to him. Louie says, That's what hit us, a damn hurricane. He smacks his hand again. Someone in the car yells, Dammit, when we goin'?

We are all grousy now about no food.

Git there soon enough, a guard yells back.

Where?

Prime Georgia countryside, boy!

They all laugh. We don't.

Louie sick to think we haven't yet managed some escape, with all the stops and transfers and what-not. I could tell him my theory but don't.

There's shouting and for a minute I am back in the Wilderness, not knowing which way to run. A boggy fear seeps up around my heart. But Gus gives me a little shake, makes sure I have blanket and coat, and then we're ordered out of the train car into sunlight strong as some explosion. Inside that light is the smell not of gunpowder but salt water.

It stirs me up, thinking transports! exchange! but then I'm scared to think it, knowing I'll be sent back for a furlough.

Yet everyone around me is larky with the idea. Except Gus. He's only watchful, like right before we crossed the Rapidan at Germania Ford. Taking in the lay of things.

Charleston, our boys are saying now.

Where it all started three years ago, when people thought it'd be over in three months.

A jumble and clutter. Rail tracks, alleys, baggage carts, wagons, teams, drovers. Louie eyeing all this. Willy too. Willy says to me, Want to try it, Jim?

I'm thinking maybe we should. Then I go a little dizzy, knowing that one step in a new direction and I'll have to keep going, chase straight through into the next thing, which will probably be the end of it all.

Gus is shaking his head. We got to stick now, he's saying. He likes this word. He has told me before that the Union has got to stick, too, and if it takes blood to make it stick, then it takes blood. But it has got to stick sure as fingers on a hand.

So if I go, he probably will too and that's what I am afraid of, above all.

This I can hardly explain to Willy, who's still looking at me, hungry to move. Why he ain't looking to Louie, I don't know, unless Louie's already set, and they just want a bunch more.

But then we're marching again, along a

corridor of guards.

What day is it? someone yells to a guard. Christmas!

Some of us look at one another, thinking, I suppose, they mean Exchange.

Then where's the eats, dammit? the fellow calls.

Turkey's straight ahead, boys. Keep moving.

So now even Louie and Willy are thinking better of running.

But Gus seems to know what's what. I see flatbed cars ahead and decide to try a joke. I say, Seems like they might be giving us a present after all.

Saying something like that make me feel a little better. Sounding like a man.

A tall fellow turns to us. Life's a festival for the wise, he says, in a deep, carrying voice.

We don't laugh.

For the lucky, I'd say, Louie offers.

The man just smiles. I'm startled, though. Seems he might be some officer. Has some sort of gravity like you sometimes find in captains and colonels and generals. But we heard they trade officers right away. They're worth a bunch of privates, for one thing, or else the rebs can get their own officers back fast.

Everything about him sags. Shoulders, eyes — The eyes give it away. Good eyes, my mother would say, but ruined by loss. She knows all about this. This fellow has a way about him like some old horse not caring if it's out in the rain or not.

One of our boys falls from the line ahead, and we all stop. A guard goes up to him, maybe says something, but nothing happens. I brace myself and then there it is, the shot.

They won't do that unless there's not much of a spark left. Even if we're half dead they can get one of theirs back.

I suppose it would be like wasting food. Otherwise.

The sun presses the cold and damp out of our bones. But the sea is far behind us somewhere, and Gus is right. We are headed straight into the heart of Secessia.

The train slows, must be a bridge ahead, and then I see two men on the embankment, and before I can think what they're doing there, one goes down in the tall grass and flowers. Shot. The other tries to run, then he's down too, just his arm coming up as if he's waving to us.

We all go quiet.

Now we can see Macon, spires and cupolas, at least somebody says it's Macon. The General, as we call him, says it looks just like a New England town so that might be where he's from. To me it looks like Montrose, up in Pennsylvania, from the hill west of town. For a time I am there again, walking down that hill, heading for the Bonhoffer house on Lake Avenue. Where all this began, for me.

Now our boys calling out familiar names. Church Street! Front Street! Court Street! And there's folks come to watch us pass. Seems we are a kind of celebration for everybody, the rebs waving back, proud, and little boys and dogs chasing the cars, a hubbub.

We try to pretend it don't bother us a bit.

Day sixteen. From the open door of this car, we see two derelict houses with no roofs to them, or windows, or doors. Beyond the houses is a swamp, dead pines sticking out of the muck and high swamp grasses dried to the color of dead cornstalks. Dogs barking somewhere.

They say it's Andersonville and there's a prison here.

Merry Christmas, one of the boys says.

And a Happy New Year to ye's.

Tonight we are bivouacking on a sandy slope. Fires and a heavy guard surround us. There's a nice breeze and from time to time we can smell the pines and hear the stream.

But Gus fit to be tied. He don't like the creeping and cringing all around, our boys all cowering because of smallpox rumors. The prison, they say, full of smallpox.

He tells us not to believe a word of it. They're stirrin' up them rumors because they don't have enough guards to keep us tethered in Secessia. Want to see us drop from fear.

We laugh a little, for him. But the General has pointed out the logic of it. *They* wouldn't be here, meaning our guards, if there was an epidemic. Besides, one Yankee stripped of weapons and equipment still equals one reb in trade so they ain't going to squander us in no epidemic.

And I am telling myself there ain't no dead line, either, which to cross it means you're dead. That's another bull of theirs.

But I wonder about it. Seems likely enough.

Well, but Gus might have something. They might be trying to weaken us sick. Keep us from even thinking about running.

I check to see if my spoon is safe. It is. I take inventory of my other items. Clasp knife, Pen, Thread and Needle, *Soldier's Book*, Boots, Blanket, Overcoat.

Seems enough to have, this minute. And above us, a bit of starry tangle.

I am grown a little numb to the old pain of it, but there's still the ambush of knowing, the all-of-a-sudden recalling that stabs out its little bivouac and then there I am, fighting that army again.

I turn on my belly.

It's not just the loss of the thing itself, that string of moments that became, for me, Gabrielle. But the whole invisible scattering of them flung out and away from her as far into time as I might have been able to go.

I look over at Gus. He's still kneeling, saying his prayers. Then he leans forward and pats the ground. Then lies down and closes his eyes and I know he is asleep.

I turn again and look up at those broken bits. Like a mirror that's been shattered beyond repair. Some great sheet of light that is now only that.

Two

Day Seventeen. We are a field of drunkards, all trying to stagger up while a guard calls us sons a'possums and a surly captain seasons each order with threats. They have commenced dividing us into messes of ninety men each. Then appoint a sergeant for each mess to take roll every morning and get our rations. The captain counts off three messes for a detachment and each one of those gets a sergeant too.

Leaves all of us shuffling about in sun and heat, with officers walking here and there grandly. Someone says there are near two thousand of us.

From this rise we see the stockade not too far off and something of the bunched-up mess within. Mouth starts shaking a bit. Gus gives me a look, so I remember to try and think of the moment under my nose. Summer heat. Hot down here, and only May. Noon, and still no grub.

Louie a nest of irritation. Still mad at himself that he did not try to run. The General tells him No way out now but through. Louie says Sounds like coward talk. Calls the General an ejeet. Calls himself that too.

25

The General takes no offense. He's still sticking close to us. Like a dog you don't want but that wants you.

Late afternoon. Going in. Going in.

Might look bad, Gus says. Don't be afraid of how something looks.

Then we're marching. Passing through gate after gate. A battlefield clamor arises. *Are we dead?* somebody says. *Is this hell?*

Gus glances back at me. We keep going until Willy up ahead stops, causing a jam. Then I am seeing it too. A surging mass of fellows belonging to no army now but their own. Gesturing and hollering. Bits of cloth hang from them. Faces and hands blackened, their shanks and arms long brown bones. Some lying in the dirt, some crawling to get close to us, trying to say things, beg for things, food, medicine, news, names of people, in all the caterwauling. Fresh fish! some of them yell. Lookit them fresh fish! Then all is a cry, and from us too. A guard shoves us forward one after another, git along, git along, git along there, no gawping! One of the skeletons latches onto my coat. I am pulling him along. Lemme me have that coat, sir! You got you a blanket now. I need that coat, sir, lookee, and I look, sickened and about to retch at the smell of him, the nakedness, the madness of his eye spilling its tears. Gus drops back, pushes the fellow away. I turn, needing to apologize, say I don't have but this coat but Gus pulling me along, as in the Wilderness. Where are we? What's this place called? someone yells, and a whinny rises up as they all laugh at us, the whole torn line of them laughing, *See fer yerselves!*

Jim, Gus says, leaning in close. Work them legs now. Keep going. Keep going.

Breath comes into me again. The sense that I have use of arms and legs, more or less, brain and heart and eyes. Am not blind, lame, sore-ridden, crazy like those others.

Was like being thrown from a horse. The ground slamming against you and breath gone and sense, and the day bursting into colors and stars. But you roll onto hands and knees and slowly get up, one part of you at a time.

Rejoin the day.

Our assigned spot is near the swamp which borders the stream running through the pen.

The swamp is a fetid sink. And so is the stream.

Men relieve themselves in the swamp

27

when they can't make it to the stream itself and the boards raised over it for a latrine. And there is much diarrhea here.

Never before have I been so conscious of the importance of wind direction.

Gus says we have to make do. Get through it. Already he is at work on our tent. While we waited for rations, we pooled greenbacks, the General and Louie did, and bought saplings from a sutler. These Gus and Louie are sinking at both ends. We'll cover them with our blankets for a tent about twelve feet long. I see that having blankets here is a kind of wealth.

And Louie planning a mud stove for us. Says he knows just how to fix it. We believe him. Has big hands, and arms to match. Ordered Willy and me to look for dry reeds. In the swamp part.

We hold our breath. Find a few handfuls of dried stuff. Run back.

I take out my spoon then put it away because the others don't have spoons.

Gus is saying Let us give thanks. The bacon-smell sea-salty. Corn pone from our oven. My head seems to float somewhere beyond me.

. . . thus far, Amen, Gus finally says, and then we're eating the bread. Made with stream water but crisp and warm at the ends, soggy and cool as pudding in the middle and tongue not wanting to lose it to the dark hollow of me.

The day eases away.

Louie saying there are eleven thousand of us in this pen of about twenty acres. And four of those swamp.

Hear these words but don't care, chewing my mouthful of bacon. A prayer, that bacon, and inside me the flame elongating, brightening, happy with its quarter-inch of new wick.

But there's an unfortunate at the edge of our light, watching our banquet. Gus sees my look, turns, then reaches over to give the fellow a bit of corn pone.

Don't encourage him, Louie says. First thing you know we'll have to put up with him.

Gus don't say nothing. The unfortunate waits for more. The General turns and gives him some of his.

Now go back to your own group, Gus says, though I can see it hurts him to say it. They'll be looking for you, he says.

We're supposed to stay among our messes and detachments in here.

Louie swears at him and the fellow departs. Then Louie tells us his plan for a well. We listen. He seems to know quite a bit about building things.

I'm thinking of those pictures in *Harper's Weekly*, the orderly rows of tents, the spirals of cook smoke. In here the thrown-together shebangs make a mockery of all that. In here it's more like the twisted black knots clumped all over some dying tree.

I say, like a fellow who's not afraid, Heard them talking of exchanges today, when me and Willy went looking for reeds.

Louie raises his big head. They're dyin', he says. That's what they mean by *exchanged*. It's a joke, son.

He goes on eating, his eyes staying blank. I look at Gus. He's considering, don't know which way to run at it.

Heat rides my face. I am back to shivering scared. I eat.

The General and I are watching the man, waiting to see what he might do. It's clear he's up to something.

There's a railing like a porch rail about fifteen feet in front of the innermost stockade, and the fellow is promenading along that railing. But he's glancing over it too. We think he's looking for something of value, and maybe we should be as well.

We must look upon Hinduism or Christianity as part of an evolving revelation that might in time be taken over into the larger religion of the spirit.

We live in an age of tension, danger and opportunity. We are aware of our insufficiencies, and can remove them if we have the vision to see the goal and the courage to work for it.

---

tinually revealing them in a new light. It combines powers of constant renewal with a firm conservancy of fundamental tradition. In Bhakti and still more in Yoga, it has perfected unrivalled techniques of mystical initiation, that contrast strongly with the frequently haphazard methods of spiritual training in the West. Above all, in the interpenetration of religion and dharma in general and the reciprocal stimulus of abstract thought and religious experiment, there is an underlying principle that, given favourable conditions, may well lead to a new integration of the human personality." *Religions of Ancient India* (1953), p. 110.

What? Buttons?

You can trade in here, for coat buttons. They're called shinnys.

He's without a shirt, without boots. His pants hang low and loose. The bones of him protrude. His dark dusty skin looks like tanned leather. Finally he crawls under the railing and kneels in the dirt. Leans forward until he's flat and grabs onto a fistful of it with each hand.

The shot comes almost at once. We look up and see the sentry on his tower. There's another shot and the fellow lies still.

The dead line, the General says. Seems clear enough.

My insides are about to rebel. The General scootches under that railing and grabs the fellow's arm. Another shot hits the dead man and not the General. He pulls him all the way out.

When a man is tired of London, the General says, he is tired of life.

I look at him.

Dr. Johnson, he says.

I have never heard of any Dr. Johnson, I say. The General, clearly, is a crazy man. Thought this right off. Everything about him slides downward. Eyes, mouth, chest. So you have to figure mind too. And those eyes too full of thought for his own good, it seems.

No letters in the dead man's pockets. No buttons, nothing.

They do that all the time, a prisoner camped nearby says. Downright dangerous, being so dang close to it.

He'll be buried in a trench, the fellow tells us. There'll be a marker board only it'll probably get stole for firewood.

We carry the dead man to the gate and put him in a row of other bodies. They tell us a wagon will take the lot out to the burial ground.

The General rubs sand on his hands, lets the sand spill down. The horrors we are seeing, he says, are proof that we've broken some moral code.

R. W. Emerson, he says.

Don't know him, neither, I say.

He looks at me. Says Just as well.

We walk back to our camp. I don't know how to think about this. And soon it dries up out of me. The whole scene. It is just plain gone and I am thinking about the General again. He is some officer, I decide, who has fooled them so as not to be traded.

It is back with me. The dead line. I hear the ball whistling so close. See the man hanging onto the dirt as if claiming it for the Union. I look up into the sky. One far-away light in a pale blue sea. Gus is reading his Bible they didn't get from him when they robbed us of near everything at Gordonsville, in Virginia. He lashed them so bad when they dropped it in the mud, they apologized and gave it back. Let me keep my book, too. It tells me now that a drunken driver on a railway can kill or maim hundreds of people. *Thou shalt do no murder.* I turn a page. Read about the breezes and gales and hurricanes. The General is reading his book, too. I don't know what it is. Louie and Will off scouting the news. Here is something. *The soul is a tree; the faculties are branches; the thoughts are buds; the words are leaves; the actions are fruit.*

Day Nineteen. Louie asked the General to write a letter for him, and they are doing that now. Nobody else among us seems to want to write to anybody. Not Gus. Not Willy. Not the General. And not me. Well, I do, only can't because I have run away and am in hiding. A good joke! So I tell myself a letter instead. Dearest Mother, I hope this letter finds you well. Though I am now a prisoner, I am neither wounded nor hurt in any way. So many of us were taken in the fighting along the Rapidan that I do not lack for company. I have made some good friends

33

and we are looking out for one another. . . .

I would not want to get her hopes up by talking of a speedy exchange being in the reb's best interest, as Louie now is.

I remember how she has told me there is not a thing that is raised but what is destroyed. Better to be a stem of grass than a maple. She told me this after I confessed to her what I had done. Which was, among other things, to ruin my employer J. L. Casey's good name and conspire in the commiting of crimes against the government of the United States.

She believes that I wanted too much and so it was only natural that it should come to ruin. My father died because he wanted too much, she believes. All that wanting causing something to burst in his head and then brain flooding over like bottom land in spring and the wash carrying him clear away. She had to work with his lawyer for months afterward, straightening out all his investments and loans. We ended up poorer than poor. But at least my grandfather did not live to see the sign coming down from our pharmacy. He had sailed from Glasgow in 1805, his pharmacopoeia books in a cedar-lined trunk. People said it was the shock of my father's death that killed him.

I tell her now that she was right about

everything except one thing. I am not yet destroyed.

Louie and the General scrabbling now over some word. The General wants a fancy one but Louie don't.

Day Twenty-one or maybe Twenty-two already. The tent without air, it seems, the raspy breathing and snorts of everybody too close. I creep out, taking my coat with me. I am sick and don't want to foul the tent. We have been drinking from the stream before our well was finished. Two holes proved dry, but the third yielded mud, then a nice seeping puddle, then our champagne. That was today, but now I am rattling with chills.

Sleeping, hunched up men everywhere, bumps darker than the night. I am careful not to fall over them. And the others, awake and sick like me.

It is a sight to make the heart pound.

Then I lose the corn pone, bacon, and all my innards, it seems. From both ends.

Mother, if I was not destroyed before, I am all but there now.

When I am empty, I creep back up to dry land and rest. I think about Louie's proposition that we build a tunnel. A tunnel! Each one of us saw how the sand spilt back into the holes when we were digging our well.

35

And who knows how far we would have to go. Louie called us ejeets. Said he counted steps on the way in while the rest of us were gaping and gawking and begging the Lord for help.

A tunnel. And what would I do then? Where would I go? Back into the army? Pick still another name? Hope for a minnie ball? Grapeshot? Well, but to be out of here, at least!

Louie thrilled as a girl with the idea. And I to blame for that, too. Told a story from the Montrose *Democrat* about an escape from Libby Prison in Richmond. Our boys there jailed up in some old tobacco warehouse. Can't even stand at the windows. Have to draw soup rations in their boots if they don't have mush-tins. But some fellows started a tunnel from the cellar. Hid it with old burlap bags by day. Tunnel led to a shed across the yard. From that shed they ducked out separately and headed down the Williamsburg Road. All they had for the work was case knives and clasp knives, a piece of rope, and a spittoon.

Louie took a vote. I abstained. Louie said he don't want no damn conscripts. All volunteers or nothing.

Gus said we should all stick. So another vote and now we go ahead.

I want to escape, but then what? This is worrisome. Want my old life back but that's dead and gone. Want Gabrielle but may as well want all them stars packed up in bushel baskets.

Right now I want not to be sick anymore.

I head back to our tent. See men creeping toward it. A bunch of them. I stay back, then I'm hollering Gus! Gus!

The General is lamenting his lost book. Today, he says, someone will be making kindling out of Plutarch.

Louie cussing, trying to fix our busted-up stove.

One blanket gone. My boots. Gus's coat. Louie's coat. The General's coat. Willy hasn't come to, yet. Sleeping at the one end, he was the first to get it.

But we found all kinds of certificates of deposit scattered around, issued by the Farmer's Bank of Elizabeth, New Jersey.

Must have fallen out of a raider's pocket.

These boys our own men. Moseby's Raiders, they're called in here.

Now we have to post guard every night.

Gus sick over it. Our own boys, he keeps saying. I am too, for it means we can trust nobody now. Neither the rebs nor our own.

The General don't seem too put out. Says

civil war is an ill-sheathed sword.

Louie tells him to stop the preachery and help him with that blasted stove.

The ground drifts closer to me, then falls away. Drifts, falls. Drifts — Chills race around me like a pack of hounds. My bones are shaking. Can't stop 'em with my mind, which is off floating over some willow-green hills, and she is saying, Do you like real music, Ira? and she is all sunset light, and somebody else is saying What have we to expect from submission? Slavery and something, something and slavery, and still we stand here, waiting, waiting. I need the swamp, need not to shame myself before Gus, Louie.

There, I fall to my knees, and after the hurricane shaking me through and through, and the wretched stillness right after, hear the click of a weapon misfiring.

The bird of thought alights and tells me that I am not a dead man yet but will be soon.

A young rebel is standing right over me, saying Git, git back, as if I am one of the mad unfortunates. Ain't supposed to be here during roll call, he's saying. Git now!

But I can't git. I wait for the sickness to roil and spill upward again and there it is, and inside it I wait for the slicing in of shot.

Dammit! he's saying. That's enough now. You get on back there! and it hits me that he's more scared than me. I git a furlough, he's saying, if I shoot you.

Then shoot, I say. Get your damn furlough.

He don't.

Who needs a dead line, I tell the others, when we got our own skin. The General rallies me, calling me a poet. I say Thank you very much. Rumors now of a true exchange. Gus advises against using the certificates to trade for boots. Thinks we could get shot for trading with contraband.

I cut lining from my coat and make bootees. The General misses his book. Pulls faces over mine. It was B. Franklin who said we have nothing to expect from submission but slavery and contempt.

I am thinking about that as I capture gray-backs and dispatch them to their heavenly reward.

Gray-backs are what we call vermin and we are all now occupied territory. It is a futile war.

A guard we bribed with a certificate leads us through the inner gate to the sick-call area between the walls. Patients lie to either side of a drainage ditch. Willy's flame hair has a white strip of bandage. He wants to go back with us. Says it smells too bad there. He don't recognize us all the way. You can see he's puzzled. The fellow next to him raises three fingers in the air. Wants something. I go over to him. What he wants is help getting on his other side. I do that while he whimpers. It disgusts me to touch him. The skin of his back comes off on my hands like old scraps of wallpaper. I get away from him quick.

Willy raves out something and a guard says Don't move him. Louie takes out another certificate. The guard ferrets it away, goes to another part of the tent, picks up a pail of waste and heaves it into the ditch, stirring up the foul broth there.

We take him back with us.

Now I sit here thinking of that fellow with the wallpaper back. How his mouth tried to make the sounds, Thanks, boy. And how it went right through me. Like I did some almighty thing. It is luny as anything to be wanting to go back there. But I do.

One of my teeth is coming loose. I am holding it in place with my tongue and worrying.

Willy still raving a little between bouts of sweaty sleep.

I get him water from our well. Sip some first.

Thanks boy, I hear, like the skritch-scratch of a file against steel.

Tonight I am on picket. Our arsenal, stones. I will doze and dream, probably, of the damn tooth falling out. Did last night.

It is day something of our captivity. Never thought I'd lose count but have.

That sickness.

And now it all feels more than ever like floating in some nothing. If I let it, fear alone could undo me. From time to time I have to look at Gus to steady myself.

He is so trim and pert, still. His straight-back white hair and dark beard. Such a small man. You'd never figure him for a veteran soldier, but he is. Told me he fought around Charleston in 'sixty-two with Stevens Brigade, then with Burnside, skirmishing around Fredericksburg. He was also in the Bull Run and Antietam battles, then his brigade was attached to Sherman's command and fought at Jackson in 'sixty-three. In east Tennessee he clashed with Mr. Longstreet, and then after walking over two hundred miles in winter, the last fifty or so barefoot, he got back to Harrisburg with the 50th and re-enlisted for another three-year term!

41

A bull? I don't think so. There is nothing mendacious about his quiet brown eyes and humble way. I believe him. What hurts is to think that he, Gus Tripp, Bradford County, Pennsylvania, is here because of me.

Son, I hear William Bonhoffer telling me again, you just don't amount up and probably never will. Not enough for her, anyhow.

Brain has become a sour mess as I watch Gus kneel down alongside his coat to say his prayers.

The soil here is either weak and slidey or else heavy clay. Cave-ins plague Louie. We begin in daylight, pretending it's a real well. We start a few holes to confuse the guards, then go back to one of 'em at night and haul away bags of dirt. Dump 'em in the swamp or in other holes. Either guards think those piles of new red dirt come from real wells, or they know what we're up to and are waiting for the enterprise to fail at this end or the other.

Saw another fellow exchange himself at the dead line. Didn't make a sound. It's like some ordinary transaction. An exchange, in fact. They give each other their freedom.

On the one hand there's that, and on the other, that fellow in the hospital saying Thanks, boy. And here I am, not knowing which way to head.

Gus and Louie a few feet away, pretending to be asleep. I take one of the mealbags Louie "bought." Slither in. It's black as black. The dirt gets colder as I move downward. Louie said Go 'till you can't no more, then start scratchin' away. How'll I know it's the right direction?

If you hit stone — or water.

It's a damn tight burrow. Eyes itch. Keep 'em shut, Louie said, but I don't. I bang knuckles against the wall. It is quiet as death in the burrow. And so still. I should not think, but I am thinking this is how it will be.

I scratch at the wall with my spoon. See bits of old bone crumbling away, the nests of underground critters. It is driving me a little luny. Think instead how it is work that will take a millennium.

All the burning and ripping up and slashing and spilling of blood don't make a lot of sense, considered from this perspective.

A fellow needs to work, Gus has told us. Work and we'll feel better.

The General piped in with, Hope is generally better than no hope.

The mealbag is a quarter full. Five bags per man, then rotate. I scratch at the wall.

Anybody there? Dirt crumbles. I scoop it up with half a canteen found at the swamp. Then more scratching.

After a while there is no thought to plague me and it is good.

Then I am thinking again. How the night I learned about Bonhoffer's blackmarket drug scheme there was no precipice, no river or ravine, nothing with which to sever or blast or drown whatever was holding the small thing that was my life to the big thing that was life and that touched other lives with its grandness. I was no more than a mush-tin. Kick it and it bangs out a sound, then lays dented and tarnished and still, a thing worth less than a brass spittoon. Unless here in camp. Here in camp, I see now, you can do something with a mush-tin, no matter how battered and tarnished. Here, it is a valuable.

But was it so wrong to believe a man you needed to believe? When he said it was all for the good? When he said our boys were suffering "down there" too, for a lack of medicines? For saying that he earned a little on the side but that wasn't the main thing? Only an incidental?

No, not wrong to believe, maybe, but the doing another matter. Specially when you do it mainly for yourself.

Ground I have been over plenty before.

This dirt damp to my touch. In my hands I feel bone, bits of skin, rotting. A man's face. I pull back, rising at the same time. Dirt skids down into my face. Then chunks. I'm flailing to create a breathing spot. Then hollering, which takes all my breath away. Gus! Louie! Sound going nowhere.

The wall is gone. The mealsack. Spoon. Canteen piece. Retreat closed off.

I holler, swallowing dirt.

Lying on my side, above the earth, I am so ashamed. I have ruined this tunnel. Louie has had to pull me out by the heels.

Louie, why in hell did you make the darn thing so worm-small. But I don't say it aloud because I am a coward.

I am no good at tunneling. No good for anything.

Resting alongside me, Gus whispers, Take hold, Jim. Take hold.

Who is Jim? I think. Then remember. It is me, too.

I am at the main gate. A volunteer, I say to the guard. For the sick-call enclosure between the gates. He gives me a close look, lets me pass without a bribe. I look for the fellow with the peeling back. He is gone.

Exchanged, they tell me.

A real exchange? I say.

Transferred, boy. He's over there now.

I go over there and see a row of bodies puffing up.

Want a job? somebody asks. An' all the whiskey you can drink?

Inside the pen, I'm running as best I can, given the terrain.

What's the news! boys holler after me. Any *news?*

Three

Ague, again. Fever and chills. Asked Willy for the India rubber pad Louie got him. He said no at first to the loan, then yes. It is fine as any bed.

Gus reads to me from his Bible, words that don't mean a thing but the sound of 'em nice. Gus, I say, I am dying. No, he says. But I am, I say, and it is all right. No it ain't, he says. And then we have a regular skirmish going. Then I go quiet and he's plagued by it. Puts a rag on my head, drags me back from wherever I am trying to go. Gus, I say, I want to. No you don't, he says. I am on a cliff, looking down at a curl of shiny ribbon. Then I'm sliding toward it, then just like that I am on the rocks again, getting ready to slide. Maybe I won't die because it is all getting too complicated. It also hits me that to give up my life now for the Union will be at least something.

I see myself writing Gus a note. These effects belong to you now. I thank you for saving me but I wish you saved yourself instead. You are worth twenty of me. Your friend, Ira Cahill Stevens.

He will wonder who that is. I have been

Jim, since knowing him.

I think how if they exchange me, I will go on making the same mistakes. This way, no. The mistakes will end. I see myself firing my ramrod into pine trees in the Wilderness, like they told us not to. I look at the pinpoints of light spilling through our tent's dark roof. Stars. No, a flare of light through bushes, and then I'm running, lost and running hard.

There's a commotion. Am I shot? I hear myself asking. Am I dead yet?

Not yet. Want to be?

I do.

That's too bad. That ain't in the plan.

It is Gus that's got me crunched against his ribs. Somebody says Ought to of let 'im go. Man's got a right.

Gus don't say a word and then we're out of range of the dead line.

Gus is intoning Behold all they that were incensed against thee shall be ashamed and confounded; they shall be as nothing, and they that strive with thee shall perish, when we hear all the shooting.

And shouting, too. Sherman! Sherman! Sherman!

Gus lowers his head, listens. Don't think so, he says.

To me it sounds like a battle striking up. We look outside. The boys are hurrahing and shouting and facing eastward.

I don't know which way to run with my thoughts, but I confess I am not a little excited. After a while a body just craves change. Good or bad.

I see all our guards taken prisoner and Capt'n Wirz hanged. I see that young guard at the stream trying to run but getting rounded up all the same. I see the stockade walls pulled down, the cookhouse pulled down, the commander's house, the sentry posts, the rubble everywhere. I see a big pine fire spitting and snapping. The fire takes up all twenty acres and leaves nothing but a black place rain comes to wash, and then a greening. I see it as if it has already happened. Sherman.

Then Louie comes in, says it ain't Sherman. Just some sham fight put on for the folks hereabouts.

Makes me riled a little. How'd you know, Louie? I say. How do you always know things ahead of everybody else?

This is how, he says, and pulls a brown loaf from his shirt.

Bread.

He tells how ladies up in the sentry posts tossed bread down into the pen. How there was trampling and stampeding to get to them loaves. How the ladies looked larky at first, then didn't. How one fainted and another screeched to be taken away.

Then Gus is saying Grace and we're all waiting. The words poke along and finally halt and we each have a piece of bread in hand. I raise it to my face. Smell wheat, butter, salt, rain, sun, the earth itself. Then I know this is what it is to be alive. Hunger burning away in the pit of you, but in your hands a perfect piece of bread.

We helped one of the unfortunates climb out of the stream. Won't last the night, probably. I sat by him a good couple of hours. Boys watching me funny, then I know why. They believe I am a Vulture, wanting something off the dying man.

I scrabble away fast. Only the most desperate steal clothing and boots.

At our tent I open my book. It tells me that no drunkard can inherit the Kingdom of God. I think to myself how no reb will either.

We hear that a Major Turner is in Andersonville right now and we are going to be paroled. A reb sergeant told me this after roll call. Others are hearing the same thing.

In my book it says despair is bad as any

disease. *Who wins the battle? The man who knows he will and vows he will.*

It don't altogether seem so to me but what do I know?

The man by the stream got me thinking about the hospital again.

In the night I ask myself who wins the battle? The man who knows he will and vows he will.

Can it be?

There's something scratching at the inside of me, wanting to tunnel out and I'm thinking maybe it is hope.

You believe a damn rebel? Louie hollers at me.

I ask him why the fellow should just come up and give such particulars.

Wants you to pass it on, Louie says.

He don't look like a lying man, I say.

Well he is.

You must want to get out of here by your tunnel is all, I say.

He and Willy go off somewhere. Willy started crying when I told him what the sergeant, Carmichael, said and how he didn't falter in the least.

I ask Gus what he thinks.

He shakes his head.

I ask the General.

51

The General slips out of his thoughts long enough to maybe hear the question but not to answer.

I am restless. Want to be doing. Want to get away from such broody fellows.

In front of our tent I walk in circles. Gus just lets me be.

I feel in my coat pocket for my book. It is there. An orderly escorts me into the hospital proper, which is an area of tents outside the stockade. The hospital is situated on an angular piece of land formed by a bend in the creek they call Sweetwater Creek. Which is a belly laugh.

The creek side is full of patrolling guards.

I have been coming here to read to the men and do whatever little things they want done when the orderlies and surgeons don't have time for them. I move them, fix bandages, give them their medicine, usually whiskey. Whiskey is the South's wonder drug.

At first I could not stand the stench from the waste buckets and drainage sink and rotting flesh. It was like walking into a solid wall of it. I thought how the stench alone must do them in. What is worse for me now is to see the gangrene. It turns limbs into slabs of rotting meat, purple and black. The flies go crazy with it all. The surgeons wear rags around their noses and mouths. The patients do not. I do not. I want to put myself in front of it all. Look and smell and take it in so that maybe that way I will drive it clear out of me. The fear and cowardliness.

On my first day a surgeon asked me if I knew what calomel was and so I told him. Merchurous chloride. A purgative. He was glad to hear I know something. Says there is one surgeon there, the greatest fool on God's earth, who prescribes calomel for whatever aches, bleeds, burns, or rots. And then diarrhea overruns the place and patients die from it. When this one prescribes, I should give the opposite of what he says, or just give whiskey.

The good surgeon is Sergeant Moore. Has clumps of wooly side hair and gray eyes that shoot light. I don't want to admit it but it is the truth. I like the man somewhat.

I kneel alongside a new patient. Tell him I have heard something about exchanges. Tell him he needs to hold on.

The fellow lets his eyes shut.

I tell him it's possible. That maybe it's not good to think everything is impossible.

He seems asleep.

I read him the Who wins the battle saying, then ask, Do you know? Who wins the battle?

Which one, he says.

Any one, I say. Battles in general.

Bobby Lee? he says.

It's the man who knows he will and vows he will, I say. Fellow named Spurgeon wrote that and I don't know who he was, but he got in this book so maybe he knew a few things.

I lean closer and real quiet ask if he thinks Grant knows he'll win and vows to win.

The fellow's eyes open. He stares up at me. Begins grimacing.

You can't say? I think he does. And maybe that's why he'll whip Lee. You watch.

His chest rises then bangs down.

A shock skitters through me. That I did him in with words, maybe.

I am weak, moving away along the row of them, scared down into my bones.

Gus has become a farmer. He is planting three whole kernels of corn found in today's ration of meal. He has made a hill on the south side of the tent, brought up who knows what fertilizer from the swamp for it, and has planted the seeds in a triangle. By summer's end, he tells me, we will be chewing on our own corn and not the rebs'.

Summer's end.

I ask if he has heard anymore about that

major in Andersonville.

He says No.

The General comes down from his clouds to say The heroic man, our culture holds, is one who persists no matter what, but elsewhere suicide is sometimes looked upon as heroic.

Gus says Enough of that kind of talk.

It is not what I need to hear right now, for I am thinking of that man I probably slayed with foolish words.

I want to sleep. In the tent I open my book and read *Thou shalt not covet thy neighbor's house, thou shalt not covet thy neighbor's wife, nor his man-servant, nor his maid-servant, nor his ox, nor his ass, nor anything that is thy neighbor's.*

So then, I think, not his freedom neither.

Quinine one hundred and eighty-eight dollars an ounce on the open market and no telling what on the black market. This an orderly tells me today. Very few drugs here, the rebs needing what they can get for their own boys. There is no morphine or morphine sulfate to dust on wounds. No opium, digitalis, belladonna. A little bromine and iodine but these closely rationed. There is calomel, also persimmons and tonics of tree-bark. There is chloroform for the amputations. Orderly today showed me a swarm of maggots feasting on a fellow's arm. It stunned me stiff and only after a while could I latch onto the words explaining why the maggots were there. Before Sergeant Moore came, orderlies had to clear off the maggots, but Sergeant Moore heard that in Napoleon's army the head surgeon discovered that maggots worked better than anything else to clean the wounds by eating away all the dead tissue. Also, they help heal somehow! So Sergeant Moore said they should stay. Don't waste the chloroform trying to get rid of them. I wash my hands with bromine and so does Sergeant Moore. The idiotic one does not, nor his saws and knives. Sergeant Moore says he is the Devil's own work.

I am thinking about how Dr. Gardner said all the medicinal plants and drugs should be taken off the contraband list and then was hissed down off the stage for saying that. William Bonhoffer showed me the newspaper article. Said that's what *he* was doing. Taking them off the contraband list where they never should have been in the first place.

And got richer doing it.

That's the sticking point.

And something says, too, that it is indeed prolonging the war.

But then so am I, maybe. Now. By helping.

I sit here broody. Thinking how we have no quinine in this place and probably never will. Thinking how once I ordered pounds of it and it probably all wound up on the black market. Thinking how I don't know anything. And all of it in my road whichever way I turn. Sergeant Moore comes by. His hand drops to my shoulder, grazes it, passing over the hump of me.

They are planking the sides and bottom of the stream, the guards, so we'll have a clean place to wash up. This new bunch is Georgia militia. Some of the others, we hear, sent to Dalton. This bunch seems decent enough.

When the boards are laid, Gus and I wait our turn, then step down into the water. If you don't look at it too closely it suffices. We don't look at how skinny we've gotten. We look instead at the balloon clouds. The puzzle of pieces they make up there.

Nothing more about that major in Andersonville.

Sherman, we hear, is only about a hundred miles away and Kilpatrick's cavalry even closer.

Gus says Jim, look there.

It is the General marching down to bathe. Like Croesus himself.

We laugh and the General with us, making no sound but his mouth wide with it.

What would I do if I were out now?

Eat. Eat something astonishingly good. Turkey, brisket, applesauce, ham, eggs, strawberries, rhubarb pie, coffee, cream, sugar.

This strikes me, at first, as the ruminations of a coward. Shouldn't a man in my predicament be thinking of doing something good or noble or worthy? That is, if not ending it all to snatch a trade from the rebs?

But I can't help thinking about eatables. Can't help thinking that maybe they are not wholly ignoble. Then I see our hills at home, all hazy after sunset, the blue pleats of them rippling away into the distance, and I am thinking I want to be back there. Just sitting there and looking. That it was foolish to run. To join up for such a snively reason. That there is something greater than pride. Greater than fear. And that, maybe, is love. If only for the earth and its things.

Seems a small thing and a large thing all at once, knowing that much, anyway. More than knowing because I knew something of this before, but now feeling it as a welling

up and almost hearing the gurgle of it.
General, I say. Strawberries!
And he says Whipped cream.
And I say Biscuits!
And he says Gravy!
And I say Rhubarb.
And he says Tart!
And I say Ham.
And he says Eggs.
And I say Apple pie.
And he says Cheese.
And on and on we go into the night.

Four

Rain.

Downpours. Showers. Curtains of mist. We rise to rain, sleep to it, eat to it — uncooked porridge. All this place smokes with rain. We sink to the ankles in mud. Gus says it is no time for the faint-hearted. So he has put us to work capturing rain water.

Sweet, going down. Almost food. Gus is calling it manna.

Our real well has collapsed into a sinkhole. And our tunnel. Louie blue, after dragging so many bags of mud to the swamp.

There was probably no Major Turner in Andersonville, ever. Another bull invented by the rebs.

The General says we should be entertained by it all for it alleviates, by diversion, the burden of time.

Louie wants to smack him.

For more trustworthy news we go to the front gate, hear it from new boys. The muddy river of us watching the clean one of them flowing in.

Some of the boys mock the new fish. The way they're scared bad like we were. I don't care for that foolery. Heavies down the heart too much. Brings it all back.

Digging again, Louie trying to make up for lost time. Digging and hauling, digging and hauling. The moon'll be full in a few days and we'll hold off. Just as well. Night work makes me too tired and then ain't much use in the hospital.

Nobody talks about afterward. I wonder if Louie's even got it plotted out. Suppose he does and is just biding time for that frosting on the cake. He's nothing but a walking plan.

Will we know which way to head? Will there be pickets in the woods? Dogs? Or will we just blow away like milkweed seeds on some night wind and nobody knowing or caring.

To think Freedom sets my heart into a quick trot and I know I'm scared. Wanting too much again.

Like some slave, maybe.

We're weakening, though. Question is, what'll go first, muscles or clasp knife?

Gus reads us about Moses in the desert, nearing the Promised Land.

The Promised Land not to be. Yet. A reb officer walked straight to our "well," kicked dirt into it, bellowed there'll be no rations until the damn thing was filled in by the rats who dug it. Louie gave us his mean look. Those camped around us suspected, probably, but nobody said a word. Rule is, any successful tunnel is public property once its owners slide through. Not that we know of any successes. Gus didn't look up from his Bible, nor the General from his book, nor me from sewing up my bootees I washed in the stream. Louie a thundercloud. The reb holstered his revolver and passed right by us. No rations! he shouted, till it's plugged up!

We still don't make a move and it is some time after the ruckus. Nobody does. Now Louie is bleak, fussing with his stove, just moving dirt around with his big hands. I don't know where Willy is.

So we go hungry. The whole twenty acres of us.

Just before sunset a reb quarter-master arrives with a gang of guards and shovels and pails, and the burrow it took us fourteen days to scrape out gets plugged tight in a little over two hours. Guards make a line leading to the swamp. Pass buckets hand to hand like putting out some fire.

Then in come the ration wagons, in the dark.

Louie says We start another one.

Gus don't say anything.

The General neither.

Then Louie says Traitor. Has to be. The reb knew straight where to go.

Strikes me as likely. If a man don't have a thing left to trade, no boots, buttons, blanket, shirt, overcoat, tobacco, sticks, rations, soap, broken stuff found down in the swamp, he can trade information. Get an extra ration. A plug of tobacco.

Don't matter even if the information is correct and true but just humbug. They give him something for it anyhow.

A mighty temptation — for a dying fellow. Maybe brave once, a good man, a patriot and Christian.

Gus says The Lord forgives.

Louie says But I don't.

Louie hooked us up with a sergeant major from Wisconsin. A new scheme. Needs perfect secrecy and coordination. Like some big battle.

Don't want to be a nay-sayer but my heart is saying it all the same.

Maybe because I am getting sick again. Diarrhea. Could be dysentery. Could be cholera.

If cholera, won't have to worry about traitors or tunnels or nothing else. Only, I don't want Gus to get it.

Our mess sergeant, who is from Pittsburgh and a Union man, is saying New uniforms, boys, and boots, full equipment, along with all the ham, eggs, biscuits, greens, succotash, and sweetbread we can stuff down our gullets. Just have to step up and sign. Join the CSA.

He don't like saying it but has to. All we have to do is sign up, boys.

Two days ago it was just uniform and equipment. Now the ante is upped.

I look down at my miserable bootees, all dried-hard mud. My belly whines and cranks. Jim, Willy says to me. I know he wants to. He talked about this last night and the one before. Well, it's hunger talking. What can it harm? he said to me. Maybe we can escape that way. Shed the uniforms and just go.

It is a point. But last night I hung back and he thought it was out of loyalty. In my book there is a story about a Scottish soldier in the Battle of Waterloo. He carried a wounded standard-bearer, colors and all, so the flag don't end up in the dirt or in enemy hands. I read Willy this story. He said that ain't got a thing to do with now. This ain't no Battle of Waterloo.

I had to agree.

Think of the raiders, he said. They're eating. They'll live.

Our mess sergeant repeats the bribe. Willy signals me with his eyes. I press fingers into my left forearm. Raise them. See indentations like in bread dough. Scurvy — for sure. A fright heaves through me like wind. If the scurvy gets my leg tendons I will not be able to walk and even the CSA won't want me. O'Ryan, the mess sergeant, is talking about the food again. I look at Gus who is standing like a man in church, the other world spelled out all over his face. I know what he is thinking. He is thinking that Grant would not do it, ever, and so won't he.

Well boys, O'Ryan says. Do I have any signers today?

Not a one of us moves. I suspect he gets an extra ration when one of our boys turns traitor. Generally they do not want to turn traitor in daylight, though. Would rather sneak over the wall at night.

Jim, Willy's eyes say again. He don't want to do it alone. What about Louie, I wonder. Louie is in his own hole, scuffling sand over his toes.

Then Gus starts it. Turns his back on O'Ryan. Just like that. Turns around as if hearing something over that way and wanting to be sure. Then we all start turning. Go ahead, I whisper to Willy. You just go and do it, if you need to.

Willy tells me I am a coward.

A shade better than a traitor, I say.

I ain't, he says. Don't you say that.

But maybe Willy is right. Maybe I am a coward.

This thought is a saddle on me and the girth too tight. I can't even be proud of being like Grant — if only for a minute and a half.

Gus reads in a carrying voice *Accursed be the hand that shall ever assail thee or take from thy heaven a single bright star.*

And we say *The star-spangled banner, the God-given banner, the blessed old banner, float on, O, float on!*

Then he says *No traitorous heart shall ever defy thee, nor hand pluck thee down from Liberty's tree.*

And we say again *The star-spangled banner, the God-given banner, &ct.*

Then he says *O, God of our fathers! Look down and protect us — This land of the brave, and this home of the free. In the day of our peril, O do not reject us, but nerve every freeman for freedom and thee!*

And we chant our words again.

On and on it goes. Gus calling out his words and we calling out ours. It all gets louder and louder as more boys join the meeting.

Now he is telling us not to fret because of evildoers, nor be envious of them. For they shall soon be cut down like the grass and wither as the green herb. Trust in the Lord and do good; so shalt thou dwell in the land, and verily thou shalt be fed.

The words pump through me, telling me the edges of things I can half believe. Where is this land we are to dwell in? What is this good I must do?

Rest in the Lord, Gus is saying. Wait patiently for Him. Fret not because of that man who brings wicked devices to pass. Cease from anger. Forsake wrath. Fret not thyself to do evil. For evildoers shall be cut off. The wicked shall not be. We'll look and look and they will not be there. And the righteous and the meek shall inherit the earth and delight themselves in the abundance of peace. The Lord laughs at the wicked. He sees that their day is coming. Their sword shall enter into their own hearts and their bows shall be broken.

Each one of us standing here wants to believe it. And for a while the words stand tree-solid in front of us and we are in the shade of its leaves and the light turns green-gold.

Then we hear a shot from the direction of the dead line.

For Gus's sake I want to believe. I want those words to be a tree for me forever. I want not to reason about nor question nor think anything. Seeing myself, I want to see no face, no eyes, no mouth, only belief. No vermin, diseases, flies, armies, states, lies, corn mush, worms, wars. Want it to rest inside me like a sun and when I raise a hand, light will shoot from my fingertips and show the way.

For the Lord loveth judgment, Gus is reading, and forsaketh not his saints. The Lord shall help them and deliver them. He shall deliver them from the wicked and save them.

Hooray for the Union! shout some of the boys. Hooray for God, Grant, and Country!

Gus is still the preacher. Now he is praying to the God of Battlefields, asking that gentle Peace come down from her home in heaven to dwell with mortals so that man shall learn war no more.

Gus and I walk back to our tent without saying anything. There we see Louie and the General playing a game of checkers in the dirt. Willy is watching.

They don't ask how the meeting was.

Crown me, Louie says and laughs his ferrety laugh.

The General tops his stick with a pebble.

Inside me the words peel away one by one and then there is just this again.

I press my forearm. Take my fingers off. It's bad.

O'Ryan telling us the new penalty for trying to escape. A cannon ball attached to leg iron and chain.

Without us to guard they could be off fighting Sherman. He and Kilpatrick are pressing in around Resaca now, we hear. I wish I was with him. Regret beginning to fill me to the gills. For not having tried to run before. That is, escape.

At the stream I tell the young guard who near shot me that he could be fighting now instead of this and how does he feel about it. Ain't you sorry? I ask him. Sherman, I say, is at Resaca now.

I don't like to gloat but there I am doing it. All the new prisoners, a thousand of them, are saying that about Sherman so it must be true. And Wirz said there's to be an exchange soon and four hundred boys were already gone. He even named Aiken's Landing on the James and Savannah, Georgia, as the places. So I am almost larky.

The guard tells me he has to be here.

Then you're like us, I tell him.

Half a hair better, he says, and spits into the stream.

I ask Gus about belief. How does it come about, Gus, that a man can believe something with his whole heart?

Gus says Well it goes like this. We get it from the Spirit and the Spirit is like something made up of all them that has gone before us and have done good things.

I say what if the Spirit don't want to give up any of it to a particular person?

And Gus says That's never the way. The Spirit always does only we are sometimes the deaf and blind ones.

And how does a person get over being blind and deaf?

He tells me the story of the blind man in the Bible whose faith saved him.

So you have to have faith first?

It all comes at once, Gus finally says. Like a downpour.

Then he says No. That ain't it, exactly. It's there already only we just have to see it.

And we are back where we started, it seems. What is hope, Gus?

Same thing, pretty much.

So you can't have one without the other?

I thought he was stumped but then he says What d'you need to grow things?

I think about it and say water and dirt.

And he says There you go.

The General tells me later that there's no talking to a religious fellow and I shouldn't tangle up my brain on it.

My mother stopped attending the Presbyterian Church of Montrose after my father died and so I stopped too. I was eleven. Since that time and now, and I am twenty, she became something of a Friend but I became mainly a heathen, I suppose, rummaging around in my woods for roots and plants and what-all for Mr. Casey's pharmacy and watching the sun slide beyond the rim of earth, slide behind the lavender pleats at day's end, and the floating up and setting of the moon, and all living things rising up and dying, in their time, and it seemed finally a good enough thing, being there in it, and I figured it was all the Church a person needed, and all the belief. But now I think there must be more to it somehow. I ask the General why is it that we must suffer.

Must? he says.

Seems that way.

So he talks, then, about moral courage and tests. How trials may be necessary and if we can withstand them, we advance our spiritual life.

Who says that? I ask.

A general theory, he says, and about as good as any.

Do you believe in it? I ask.

He looks at me, his bookish man's eyes full and sad.

Sometimes, he says.

What about the rest of the time?

Oh, I believe we live and we die.

Don't sound like much.

And he says, Well it ain't.

What I thought, too, I see now. Only there are two ways of seeing it, clearly. Good and bad.

Richmond, the guard at the stream tells me, looks like a gone-up case.

How d'you know that?

Person hears.

Is Grant there already?

Don't matter if he ain't right now, it's done.

You from there?

Farm up in the Cumberland. My wife wrote we got burnt out. She and the boys are with her mama. Don't know about the crops. Gone, probably. She said the Yankees took the stock and fired the barn, house, apple trees. Every last thing they could.

He is smaller than me in height and looks no older, but there he is talking like a man. Man with a wife and children and farm.

You want to be back there now? I say.

Don't know. Don't want to see it, I do know.

Might not be so bad.

It's bad. It's all gone.

If you shot me, you could have got yourself a furlough.

And we'd both be better off, maybe.

Well you still can, I say.

Start runnin'.

Start shootin'.

We look at one another. Then he smiles a little. Spits tobacco juice at the water.

She don't know I'm here, he says. Thinks I'm with Johnston. I make things up to tell her.

What kinds of things?

Oh, like I'm in different places and we're pressing hard against Sherman.

But he ain't? — Johnston?

Not supposed to say.

I take some mud and start rubbing at my feet. Find it humorous. Mud to clean off mud.

I can get you some soap, he says. Only don't tell where you got it.

I can't say the words *thank you* all of a sudden, but I nod. Then look over at the big pile of cloud rising above the pines to the east. White and pink and all furbelowed.

My name's Harley, the guard says. What's yours?

Ira, I say. Ira Cahill Stevens.

I don't know why but I begin to feel very much depressed in spirit. Not because I told him my true name but because the fellow seems so much better than me. Not better off. Just plain better. More maybe than I will ever be. For I started out just plain wanting to hurt him.

Our second "well" has been discovered — and filled in by rebs. Louie is telling us that it has to be some informer. Gus is of the opinion that it is a spy. Somebody awake and watching. If I catch him, Louie says, he will be a dead spy.

Louie wants to move operations way over to the other side of the pen. I say maybe we should wait a bit. Louie asks if I'm scared of a ball and chain. He laughs. All we need to do is get a hacksaw somehow. Saw the thing off, cobble it together for roll call.

Gus closes our little session with a prayer. Courage brother! do not stumble, though thy path is dark as night, there's a star to guide the humble. Trust in God and do the right.

But let's keep working, Louie says, while we're trustin'. Then he says Boys, the Lord just lit up the road.

We all feel his excitement. Be like that, I'm thinking, as we vote to stick with him. Prayer is one thing, Louie's hands another and maybe the stronger of the two.

What am I reading? the General wants to know, so I read it to him. *Happy whoso learneth here from the nothingness of this life, and looketh through its vapors to the realities of the life to come.*

The General says I'd say he got the vapors part right. As for the nothingness, the fellow probably never spent a minute as a prisoner of war.

Is this going to elude us, too? I ask. Our new scheme?

Only the God of Battles knows, says the General.

There is no talking to the man and getting a decent answer.

Saw him stooping and muttering to a man lying on the ground the other day. Life is indeed plenty, he said. Plenty of regret, bad judgment, selfish dreams of grandeur, and puny scheming wrung out of brains less worthy than those of a cow.

And the man on the ground said Ain't no cows in here, and that's a fact.

Cloud shadows now, racing north to south.

I am a little blue so take out my effects and line them up before me. Book. Thread. Needle. Pen. Clasp knife.

It's something, I tell myself, and not nothing. Keep going, Ira. Keep going. For despondency is the abandonment of good and the giving up of the battle of life with dead nothingness.

But it would be nice to know, anyway, what day it is.

Everything that rises is destroyed. Louie no longer a proud man. He had crews of fellows digging tunnels all along the west stockade, our plan not to escape by underground but above. These walls were supposed to tumble at the trumpet's blast. Instead the cursed rebs walked straight to each and every hole and it is the same story all over again. Informers. Or maybe just one. The Captain nailed up a notice at the main gate warning us all that he knows everything and if anyone at all makes the least suspicious move, he is going to grape and cannister the whole lot of us until there ain't a man left kicking.

The informer must not have given Louie's name or else they'd surely have him hanged by now or at least in leg irons.

We hear that some seven hundred men from Grant's army have come in. Taken around Chancellorsville and robbed of most everything.

Louie just robbed us of one blanket from the tent. He is going off to find some whiskey. Needs a spree. We let him go without a word of protest.

We just don't understand it. We thought the plan was big enough to outdo even the smallest, meanest informer.

Well, but it wasn't.

Five

A fellow drags his cannonball and chain into the stream and splashes water over himself. On the bank others lay in foulness. I sit on a clear patch, awaiting the next attack. But in the meantime I study the clouds. Reflect on how it is good the rebs at least can't take these from us. Today they look like cream-colored flowers. What if they are gods, looking down on all this, then just sailing their way?

Oh Ira, where have you got to now, in your luny brain?

The attack comes and I don't see much of anything. Fear floods the little plains and valleys and hills of me.

Somebody asks how I am. I open my eyes and see the General. Don't get close, I say. But he sits a few feet away.

Sometimes it seems you don't care about anything one way or another, I say. Is that fair to say?

No, he says. But he don't say any more. Then he wanders off and I feel bad I chased him away. In the stream I lose the bit of soap Harley gave me and have something real to feel bad about.

Sixteen hundred new prisoners in two days, we hear. But if there is some exchange, they might trade us first, seeing as how we're getting less and less fit each day and are certainly worse off than these new boys. The new ones shy away from us. Keep to themselves.

Willy torturing us with his ravings and sinking spells.

Jim, the General says. Hear Wirz is digging his own trench now — to stop the tunnels. Good joke, eh? We dig. They dig. It is the General's way of trying to rally me.

Teeth banging against one another and I believe they mean to fall out. The General stays with me instead of digging. I wake and sleep, wake and sleep, and he is always there. I want to tell him it's good, the furnace of heat he is when I am at my North Pole. Then they come in, Louie, Gus, Willy, and Louie is saying But what we need is some first-rate hangings. Gagging and bucking's too good for them.

Gagging and bucking. That means they catch raiders, shave one side of their heads, and push them down in the muck at the swamp. I am seeing this, then I am the person, then the General fixes the rag on my forehead, pulling me out of it. I ask him his name. Marinus Bittner, he says.

Marinus, I say. I thank you.

I understand why he stays in the tent with me. On account of raiders. He has also cleaned up my foulness and I am ashamed. Not so much of that for it is only natural, but for seeing the fellow only as some stray dog. How is it that we put ourselves above others? Why do we need to? Is it fear? Is it smallness?

Then all thoughts bust up in the storm.

Am walking again. Saw raiders gagged and bucked, down at the stream. Couldn't watch for long. Louie says it stops 'em for a while.

The camp on alert now. Reb working parties pulled in, we hear. Sharpshooters at their posts. Guns everywhere turned outward. We have our effects tied to us in case it's Sherman. Nobody knows now what will happen next.

Came to naught. Instead, a thousand new prisoners come in — from Grant's army and Siegal's corps in the Shenandoah.

When hope leaves a fellow too fast, you all but collapse.

Another thousand. Butler's. Robbed real bad. Rebs now building fires around the inside. Pickets stand behind them and have to look at us through the flames. We can see them; they see us? Nobody ever escaped here by a tunnel, we hear. Plug of tobacco enough to undo weeks of work.

Work started again but we hit something. To cut left or right puts us too close to the sentries. Everybody scared of what else we might run into if we keep mousing in that place.

Heavy rain today.

Rain. Tent dripping inside. Another right smart shower, as they say here. Low cloud. Fog. Men lying in the wet. Cave-ins. Louie sore about everything. Willy complains of headache. We're bunched up in here and it's aggravating.

Clouds thinning. A bit of sun. This whole side of the camp out cheering. We got a small fire going with roots we kept dry under our shirts. When I stand too fast or bend forward too fast, I go blind and dizzy. Fainting might pass the time, Gus says, if only a fellow could be sure of not being robbed.

Vermin have upper hand.

Stream running high and fast, churning away all the filth.

★ ★ ★

News! Fort Darling fallen! Grant broke Lee's center at Mechanicsville! New men swear to this. I tell Marinus I'm scared to believe anything anymore. He responds with his entertainment theory. How it exercises the brain so long as we don't take it too seriously. How can we not? I say. Well, he says, the least action affects everything and so everything is important but you don't want to drive yourself mad.

This don't square with what I observed about the man. Now he's saying everything's important when sometimes he acts just the opposite.

Rebs treating Negro prisoners fairly well. They go outside the stockade on wood detail or to fix the walls. Then they get extra rations. They can buy things on the outside and sell it for more inside. Add to rain, sickness, hunger, this envy now.

Some entertainment.

Today Willy tells us Mary Ann has blue eyes the color of a China doll's. We don't know who Mary Ann is, but she has five sisters and they all sing in a choir. She lives in a white house with a black iron fence around it. Yesterday she lived on a big dairy farm. Tomorrow she will probably be the mistress of a school and have black hair and green eyes. We all feel sorry for Willy but don't know what to do for him.

More rain now. Rebs ringing us 'round with fires.

Gus says Where there's smoke, &ct. Lightning shows us our leaky ceiling. Thunder booms like heavy artillery. Makes us all depressed of spirit, hearing those battle sounds which don't have a thing to do with us. The world in its own fight.

Rain. Blows over the camp in gray curtains, brown torn curtains. Then fog and showers, showers and downpours and mists. We are sinking in mud again. Roll calls a sham, men answering for other men and nobody checking. The rebs' fires out. Ours too. Ration wagons always late, mules, wagons, mealsacks black with wet, and all of us, prisoners and guards alike dripping and weighted and cussing. Our stove dissolved. When you going to start? Marinus asked Gus on the fifth straight day of rain. Start what? Gus said. Building your ark, Marinus said.

There is no place to get away from one another. The best thing is not to talk at all. Not about our caved-in tunnel, not about the new rumors of exchange flickering even

in this rain, not about how the Negro prisoners are faring under the rebs.

I could kill 'em, Louie says.

That's what they want, Gus says. Set us
apart one from the other, divide us further.

What's the good of it now? Louie says.

Gus says Just teach us a lesson and have
fun along the way.

They shouldn't do it, Louie says, meaning
the Negroes.

Well, they're starving too, Gus says.

Willy holds his hands to his head.

Louie takes his pillow, a mealsack, and
shoves it under Willy's head.

Marinus brings in the mush-tin filled with
rainwater and we pass it around, drink until
it's all gone.

We figure it's still June. The word seems
funny. June. June. June. Junejunejunejuneju

All words do. And every single thought
you can hold in your head. Every lick of
sense running off downhill.

Exchange! The 51st Virginia coming to
guard us!

Richmond evacuated! Lee at Danville!
Kilpatrick's cavalry rampaging around
Augusta!

Gusting humid air swirls these rumors,
then Marinus comes upon a page of swirling

newspaper, the *Charleston Mercury*. Editorial says the Confederacy shouldn't put forth any peace propositions now because it might make them seem weak.

We add the exclamation point. Ergo, Marinus says for our entertainment, they are weak and want to conceal the fact. Or they aren't and don't want to seem so. Or some of them do want peace and others of them don't.

Thoughts swirling, fermenting. Gus digs run-off channels around his corn. Louie tells us They're saying they're going to retaliate by killing a thousand of us because our government is talking of doing the same. Marinus tells him he's just like Grant at Vicksburg last year. Bogged down in all the mud.

Sure, Gus says, but he made it through, didn't he?

And now it's raining again.

An order comes down to take all the sick and dying to the main gate. Louie says Willy's not going.

Gus wonders if they're taking all the sick to some decent hospital somewhere and maybe it might be a good thing.

No, Louie says, all the same. He ain't going.

We're jailed up again inside. Gus tells us

God won't ever be on the side of a government that treats men like this. Marinus says God don't take sides, it's all one to him. How d'you know? Gus says. How d'you know what He's thinking or not? To break up the fight I tell about what I heard. Six Negroes overpowering their guards on a wood detail, then escaping and so far not caught. Louie fidgets. Gus is quiet. They tried to get on the firewood squads and were told they are too old. I did too. But I am too weak and Willy too young. Only Marinus didn't even try. Louie says it's probably not even true about those Negroes getting away. Then Willy says It is true, and Louie gives him a look. How d'you know that? And Willy says Heard them talking about it, the rebs. The rebs? Louie says. Where'd you hear them talking? And then Willy don't say anything more. I say, to break the spell, imagine being in the woods again. And smelling the pines up close. Fellow just might faint. Gus says Probably would anyhow, carrying all that wood. Then nobody says anything again, and Willy's just sitting there and then Marinus tells of a big oak shot to bits at Spottsylvania, in Virginia, a place they are calling the Bloody Angle. How come, he asks us, we can't make even the plainest of weeds but can blast to atoms trees and every other thing in this world? We don't have any answer for him. But I am thinking It can't be Willy.

He must be a Confederate, only it's not immediately clear because he's in dandy civilian clothing. He stands on a stump, addressing us. Do we want to come and work in a rebel boot factory?

Are you making boots for Jeff Davis? a prisoner yells.

Well yes they are, the fellow says politely, but also for other citizens, including women and children. He promises to feed us well. Get us medicines if we're sick. They need workers; we need food. And wouldn't it be a fine thing to have some useful work to do?

How come you don't sound like no rebel? someone yells, and we recognize Louie's voice.

The man tells us about living in Philadelphia as a youngster. This is all Louie needs to hear. In the next minute the fellow is in Louie's strangle-hold and two other fellows are holding him as well, and out comes a razor and in no time all the man's yellow-white hair is gone, the man yelping to high heaven. Guards swing by, laughing. Haul the man out of the dirt, tell him he was plain lucky to be spared the swamp. They hurry the dandy away through the camp, the bunch of us hooting.

But he seemed a decent sort. Even if he did have too-shiny boots.

At least a hundred of us died today.

Be thou propitious, Caesar, guide my course/And to my bold endeavors add Thy force. A poem Marinus recites for us. *Pity the poet's and the plowman's cares/Interest Thy greatness in our mean affairs/And use Thyself betimes to hear and grant our prayers.* Gus likes the word *grant* in there. Says to take out Caesar's name and put in Grant's. They are squabbling about that now. Marinus says it already means that and Gus should be able to figure it out, seeing how he feels about Grant. Marinus then goes and spoils it by adding how Grant can hardly figure out his own course, let alone ours. Gus sore.

At least a hundred more of us dead.

I read from my book. *Courage consists not in acting without fear but being resolute in a just cause.* Plutarch wrote that. I tell Marinus. He says Sounds like him. We end up talking about politics and I tell him Mr. Casey's theory. That politics is just the strong being able to do legally what they wanted to do in the first place, right or wrong. Marinus don't exactly smile, but you can tell he's pleased by the way he winks a little and his mouth twists up at one end. Then he's telling me something that seems some different language. How politics is only one part of it but not enough to get at the invisible thing you feel like a wound under the skin. That Which Is Never Enough, he calls this wound, if I am getting it all straight. I ask if he was a preacher before. He says No. I ask if he thinks doubt is a gangrene of the soul. He winks a little. The mouth twitches upward. Then he says that sometime doubt is good. Keeps us humble, where we belong.

Like the maggots, I tell him.

There is so much time to fill. We float in it, cast-aways adrift, lost, forgotten. We can look up straight into the sky and all that is the time we must fill.

It is a nonsensical thing, but I have hope.

Rumors skittering. Three hundred new prisoners taken near Petersburg! New York *Herald* says exchanges to commence July 7! Transports leaving New York for Savannah! Guards going on furlough in three weeks because all of us to be gone! CSA General Winder to square up with prisoners for all lost goods!

A bull, Louie says. All a bull.

Marinus starts preaching again, in his way, about how we are the incarnation of Winder's choice, Wirz's choice, Bobby Lee's choice. They chose, and now their choice half scares them to death. Not to choose is to have everything and nothing, all possibility. Pick something, and you have to live with it and know you can't go back and pick again. No wonder they don't like looking at the lot of us.

It don't work like that, Louie says. You can pick again.

No, Marinus says. Not in this.

Sure! Louie says, a thing don't work out, you just go on.

Not in the big things, Marinus says.

Another bull, Louie says.

Boys, Gus says, guard my corn close tonight.

Marinus, says Going blindly on don't preclude —

And Louie says, A bee in your noddle, them shell-games and what-not. Thing to do is to pick and if it's wrong, hell, pick again. Man has all kinds of chances.

We talk for a while about our boys getting into Lynchburg and burning warehouses but not able to take the place. We talk about the new extension the rebs are supposed to be building onto this place.

Gus halts that talk. We try for sleep. But I am thinking about choices. Son, Bonhoffer is saying to me, you didn't tell me you worked for J. L. Casey, and I am saying again I thought you knew, sir, and he says Well that puts a different slant on it, don't it? And I don't know how to answer that, so I stand in his study, waiting, and then he says She's in the music room, practicing. I believe she's at it too much for her own good. Maybe we can talk a while and then you might go in and say hello. And then he's saying It's good to do a right thing, ain't it? And I push aside What is the good? and walk into the music room and only nod, because she's playing, and I sit down on a creaky chair, and a thought charges all through me — how hard it all is, finally, and so, maybe, not the right thing after all. And the silky tangle of music threading me up all the more.

Another thousand in today, and a small dog happy and friendly as anything.

I fall asleep thinking of that little dog. In here.

I am sitting near a dying man at the stream, and I hear myself saying Sir, you promise those boots to anyone?

And he says You mean you want 'em. Git away, snake. I say I can help him. If he wants a bath, I'll help him do that. That's what I meant. He says No you don't. Git.

I watch him skitter himself down bit by bit to the water. I tell myself it ain't a crime, what I'm doing. I should be at the hospital but I stay here, on guard. If I don't, somebody else'll get them boots.

He is still here, the dying man. Other boys, too, waiting for the end. I have come to apologize and I tell him so. He tries to laugh. I ain't a raider, I tell him.

The third day and he is not dead yet. I bring him drinking water from our well. He says to me Take 'em. Know you want 'em. I tell him I don't anymore. Don't lie, he says. I say I did want 'em but don't now and it's the truth. Then I say No it ain't. It's half a lie. He says You can have 'em, only make sure I get buried deep enough and say a prayer. He tries to sit up. I tell him to give the boots to one of the other boys. No, he says. Don't fight me now. He is nothing but a string of bones. Then he tries to get the left boot off but don't have the strength. I have to help him do that.

He's gone now and I have the boots. Calfskin. Initials stitched into the top of each. TRS They're too narrow. Hurt, so had to cut them open with my knife though I hated doing that. We said a prayer for him from Gus's Bible. Don't know if he was buried deep enough.

A fellow asleep in his tent was buried in a "well" cave-in. Another in a shebang near the dead line was accidentally shot. Orderly at the hospital says the CSA's nearly played out. Also, rain's ruined the wheat this year. Bad news for us. The fellow is going to desert soon as our army crosses the Chattahoochee, he says.

It don't brace me up. All these sixes and sevens.

Our cavalry somewhere close — a rumor. Two hundred new boys coming in. From Gen. Sturgis. Same story. He was near dead drunk again and got them all in a fix. Only as many as die in the hospital are let in.

Even when I don't want to hope, I do.

Today, Marinus asked me if I have ever loved anyone. Meaning a young lady. I lied, said no. He asked if I ever killed a man. I didn't lie, said no. He said some things kill worse than shot and powder. What? I said. He said Words. What does that mean? I said. Oh, for instance — A brother declares his sister insane, gets a judge to agree, order her to an asylum, then gets the sister's land.

Ain't that a kind of — Death? Wouldn't you call that breaking the spirit of the law? Said I didn't know. His talking mood played out. He looked at my boots. Didn't ask about them. I was shamed nonetheless.

Rice and poor beef for dinner.

Am thinking about the for instance he gave. Whether he's the brother or the judge. Or whether it was just his sort of talk.

I am cooking beans I traded a certificate for. They simmer in our well water. No carrot or onion, but still a heaven. I am doing this for the others not myself because I do not deserve a one of them.

Going to the hospital today, I fell in with a stampede of boys, Louie among them. Seemed we might be running for something — freedom, maybe. Louie shouted Jim! Jim! And so I followed him, not seeing at first the wagon-spoke clubs the boys were wielding. Then I did. And also saw the half-shaved boys dragged out of shebangs and even wells and drawn into the bunch of us.

At the central gate, rebs took them from us, the boys shouting Hang 'em! Shoot 'em! But then the gate opened again, and the raiders were shoved out into the mob of us.

We broke into two ragged lines and commenced pounding those boys. I did so too.

Raised my fist, felt it striking again and again, the pain of it spinning up my arm and pouring all through me. Some yelled they were innocent, but we hit them anyway. I won't say I wasn't myself. For there I was, bad as all the rest.

The boys we hit tried to get away from us but ended up in a big pile and then got kicked and beaten some more. One boy looked right at me, his face split down one side like pink upholstery that had sprung apart.

It sickened me to my depths. Not him. But me, myself.

So I stayed there with him until he was gone. And the mob. A passing reb dropped a chunk of firewood. A prisoner came by to loot the pile, spied the wood. Called me an ejeet for not picking it up. Eye for an eye, this fellow said. You gone crazy, boy? Where you gonna find a nice piece a wood like that in here?

He's got that wood now.

I pass the beans around, fat and sizzling. Splitting along the side. I don't eat.

Louie says it's good of me. Calls me a good cook.

I don't answer him. He says The boy ain't gonna talk now. Jim, you're crazy to take it bad. They got their due. Lookit what they did to Will. Stop moping over it. Eat some of those beans. You'll feel better.

Let him be, Marinus says.

Listen to the General, Louie mocks. He done better than you, sir. Least he done something.

Boys, Gus says. Let's enjoy these beans.

But Louie is on his horse. When a man's got something to contribute to the cause, Louie says, he owes it. Whether hands or brains.

Louie sore at Marinus because Marinus won't be a judge for them, in the trials of the raiders.

Refusing to serve is a cowardly act, sir. A treasonable act, Louie pontificates.

Pay some heed to these beans, Gus says.

Fellow lost his watch to 'em, Louie goes on. And they nearly brained him too. And now they're even getting attorneys! Don't you want this place to be safer?

Marinus says, So convenient a thing it is to be a reasonable creature.

Think you know everything, Louie says. Don't you? But what if them raiders brained that fine head of yours?

I only half listen to their squabble. Am swelling up with stones inside. Feet, legs, belly, hands, arms, chest, head. Can't breathe without I'll burst. Heart a hare caught in a wire fence, trying to push through.

Early star low in the east, where Sherman might be. Resolute in his own cause. Which is to beat Johnston maybe. In here trials going on and Louie strutting from place to place. Willy going down fast in his brain. Marinus broody and sad. I am becoming one of the shadows, as they're called. Gus has called a bucking-up meeting.

This evening he is preaching on the First and Greatest Commandment and the Second which is like unto it. Thou shalt love the Lord thy God with thy whole heart, and with thy whole soul, and with thy whole mind. And thou shalt love thy neighbor as thyself. I am wondering how he is going to square that with the idea of your neighbor being a reb. Or a raider.

He don't. But boys go up to profess all the same. I don't.

Now he's saying We must rise in our strength and pride and crush their mimic throne. Meaning Satan's and the CSA.

Ain't strength and pride what does us in? I wonder. And how is it that if you love your flag, you hate your neighbor's? And if you love your neighbor or a few neighbors, you hate other folks?

Very much depressed in spirit. Broody. Which shows me to be but weak and miserable. No use to myself or most others. Except maybe my dying boys.

Wiry Gus comes up to me. Wraps me around in his arms just as he done in the Wilderness, and I stand there in the circle of him limp as some lamb born in a big spring blow.

Only I ain't no lamb and that's for sure.

Six

July, we think. More round-ups. I am staying out of it. Rebs brought in a raider called Limber Jim and some of his gang and they led straight to the rest of their bunch. Found under tents: money, watches, knives, pistols. Evidence for the trials. Believe the rebs know better than to set Limber Jim loose among us. Fox for the dogs.

Surgeons have deserted the hospital. Or else ordered somewhere else. I am giving myself over to the work there. Try to help those miserables rather than squalor in my own misery all the time.

Believe I am seeing something and it is this. We cannot reverence God the Creator without reverencing His creatures, all of 'em, even the rebels, even the raiders, even the brutes, the vermin. Hard as that is to stomach. Otherwise, we lie down in shame and our confusion covers us. In everything is the flame of life. To know this is one thing. To be truly sensible of it, another.

The words *the 7th* pass man to man with the greatest reverence. Exchanges to commence on that day, we hear. Also hear folks up North are holding indignation meetings and sending petitions to Congress to hasten exchanges.

It is hard to wait with hope. But harder without it. Hardest of all is to be a battlefield, the slashing and cutting all inside. Now one side winning, now the other.

Standing near his tall corn, Gus is telling us that we are the footprints of history. Our first duty, therefore, is to live. Take care of ourselves body and spirit and also each other. But if we can run, we should and then bear witness. Whatever befalls us, our running will be proof of loving our neighbors here. Christ so loved the world that He laid down His life, &ct.

Marinus silent at these meetings. Louie and Willy usually absent.

Gus says we should pray regularly to our heavenly commander-in-chief. Marinus winked at that. We both know that for Gus the heavenly commander wears a Federal private's shirt with shoulder belt, a slouch hat and dusty boots, has a beard and smokes cigars.

The rebs surrendering no food today. Not an ounce. Too busy organizing skeletons.

Some are saying it is July 4. The Glorious Fourth. Will Grant take Richmond today? Last year Vicksburg fell to us. And Gettysburg.

And last year Gabrielle and her sisters played their fiddles on a stage set up in the middle of the green. Wind moving through everything, scattering sheet music, and through me as well, hollowed out, there in the spindly shade. It was when the wanting started, and all this, too.

I do not understand time. How a snag of sticks, or a few stones can alter its course. I think of Stonewall accidentally shot by his own men. Or the Wilderness for that matter. Who can control it? Any of it? I tell Marinus this and he says An argument for despair, then, don't you think?

I say Why always see the dark of it?

Well, he says, because it's all dark. Then he laughs and says I should think what I want to because my spirit is free.

Seems he has given up the fight long ago but why he hangs on here with us I cannot fathom.

We come to a man who won't eat. He's old. His lips are stuck flat down against each other and he won't open his mouth for Kingdom Come. A younger fellow is trying to poke in some watery cornmeal. The older one blows it away. The younger one says I believe my Father has gone off his head. This is the third day he won't eat. Marinus

101

leans to whisper something to the younger one.

What did you say? I ask him later. Marinus says To let him be. Not badger him.

Seems right, don't it? I am thinking now. And all those in the hospital, don't badger, spare yourself, let 'em be. No more seeing flesh bursting from the bloat of dropsy, or diarrhea that is nothing but blood, or skin purple and rotted as rain-soaked wallpaper.

I go into the tent and Willy is there, choking, nearly, on tears. In one of these fits, he don't hear us. So I lay down nearby and just let it drum, like rain. Say to myself, don't badger. Let everything be.

Feels like floating nowhere. Feels like death itself.

Then Louie's hollering Come on out here, you weepy wimmen. Don't you know it's the Fourth of July!

We hear blasting and hooing. Willy stops crying.

I give up being dead in favor of percussion caps and ten-penny nails and pieces of brick.

Hurrah boys! some of us shouting. Hurrah for the Union now and forever.

A grand racket.

We spend most of the Glorious Fourth being counted and recounted, the rebs not wanting us to have our day. We have a new number. Twenty-three. Don't know what it means, whether fair or ill.

One rumor has proven true. A bigger pen. And we ourselves contributing to the odious work. Though for us, not entirely odious. Louie comes up with another of his madman's schemes and we go barmy with him. He has rope and a carpenter's saw and he is not the only one. Scores of boys do, and the first thing we know, there goes the dead line. Trampled! Busted up! Firewood! Then the innermost wall is pulled down and the rebs allowing this. We hear the crackling and splintering and give a great cheer. Some of us are hollering Work fast, boys! They'll stop us any minute. Others holler A bull! What do they care? Boys, listen! someone else calls. Severe penalties for destroying CSA property. But the pulling, splintering, sawing, crashing, stomping, and dragging-away of CSA property goes on. Posts, boards, sentry boxes, ramparts, buttresses rendered into stove wood and kindling, and the sap smell of fresh-sawn pinewood rising up in the night, and guards on their distant perches knowing, from all the racket, but not caring in the least. Which, of the whole strange night, seems strangest of all.

The wall comes down and we see, beyond it, another one, as in some dream. With its own dead line already in place.

And now, too, firewood to guard.

I believe that I now can say I know somebody who lives by the Second Commandment. A priest comes into the stockade to minister to the Roman Catholic boys, and I'm considering lying and saying that I am one too — if only I could keep it from Gus. Don't know as it is so important what he says, preaching all sounding much the same, but what he does — and how he looks. He is rugged, not a frail flower. Irish, and it might be his nose was broken once. There is a scar running deep through one eyebrow. He is always reining in his deep voice. Part of me wants to believe he is one of Sherman's aides come to spy out the lay of the land. He ain't a bit disgusted by how we look nor is he afraid to get too close. Even the surgeons prescribe from a distance, but this man will put an arm right around a fellow or sit alongside him, and he don't spout too many holy words, either, from what I can hear. Just asks a boy how he's feeling, where he's from, and if he has any letters to be sent. He rigs up bandages from scraps or else gets water or just listens to the crazy ones. The Romans call him Father Blaze.

At the stream he spied me trying to wash my hair and came over. Told me of an old remedy — mud plaster. Called me a man with a million and laughed. I warned him about getting close. He said I took a vow of poverty, son. They won't stick to me. Then commenced to plaster the critters, saying he was sorry for them, only doing what was in them to do, but when it's a question of being under siege, then it's a matter of self-defense, ain't it?

I pulled back a little, thinking how he was just a reb defending the rebels. Then he asked where I'm from and what I did before and I was back there again, in Montrose, in the shop now Mr. Casey's, his sign swinging outside. *Dealer in Drugs, Chemicals, Dye Stuffs, Paints, Glass Ware, Groceries, Fancy Goods, Jewelry, &tc.* And remembering the day he took our old sign down, *Manley Stevens & Son*, then tore down the wall between our shop and another to make everything his and everything new. And I'm seeing the drawers and bins, the jars and packets I worked with for so long, he decent enough to keep me on, and the lithographs and stoneware, the buggy whips and lamp oil, and her coming into the shop, Do you like music, Ira? and I am weeping bad as Willy.

He put me into a fighter's hold and hung on while I gusted away and then just stopped dead. Told me I'll be back there before long. But first I have to believe I will. That's the main thing. Belief. So I asked him about the 7th. Is there to be an exchange? He went secretive. Rinsed his hands. Can't say, he said. Ain't allowed. Asked him about Grant, if he's whipping Lee, just nod. He shook his head. Did I want to confess any sins? I told him I ain't Roman.

Ah well, a blessing for you anyhow. And off he went on creaky knees.

Now I am trying to puzzle it out. Any aide for Sherman would have said it straight out. Marinus says not to get hopes up. He is only a priest.

A knife slash couldn't feel any worse. The burn and pulsing of it. That is hope doing its work. And each time I hear *the 7th* the ache leaps into life as if struck.

Three to four hundred more prisoners coming in now. The novelty has worn off for me. I do not rush to the gate to see them as lots of boys do, to mimic their surprise. Seems a cruel practice. Louie always goes. He would make a fine investigator or spy.

Today he learned that these new boys are mainly from the Danville, Virginia, fighting. They have been tearing up railroad. They heat the rails afterward and twist them like ribbons around nearby trees. Seems that is all we know how to do. Rip and tear and ruin. Louie in high spirits. Richmond completely surrounded, he says. Fighting there day and night. Grant getting upper hand. Speare's cavalry sweeping back and forth around Danville.

But I don't know. Marinus will not say what he thinks about tomorrow. Tells me not to torture myself so much. The book he is now reading is by Marcus Aurelius. Got it from a sutler, probably. Gus worries me more. Mumbling about moments big with blessing and every so often diving into that Bible of his, searching out verses and planning what he is going to say to us. He has become popular now. But I am somewhat cold on all those words. With me it is the sharp blade of hope doing its work. And when the blade gets pulled out, it's worse. Sometimes I'd rather be anyone but myself. No, that is not true. I do not want to be those putrefying in the hospital. Nor that dying man who refused to eat. I ask myself how Father Blaze would think but then remember that he is free.

Gus's prayer meeting a success. Nearly a hundred boys. He convinced most that this time tomorrow we will all be on transports. Read us verses about Moses and Pharoah, then told us jokes, one about a sailor who was assigned to a coastal battery and had to ride a horse. Well he couldn't, not for the life of him, and kept falling off. The commanding officer said to him What did you enlist for? The sailor said To shoot secessionists, not break colts. After the laughter fell away, Gus went on, telling us of some editorial giving the rebs' terms for peace. First we have to acknowledge their right to secede, pay all the costs of the fight and all the damage, and finally have to indict and hang President Lincoln. What d'you think of that?

Hoots.

Thought so, Gus says. Well, the way I figure, that's like saying God should acknowledge old Satan's right to rebel, give him a fat reward for so doing, turn the universe over to him, and then go shoot Himself.

Laughter. Applause.

The way to peace is to fight clear through to it, like the Israelites in the desert, fighting their way through every adversity. Like General U. S. Grant. Each man of us can still fight. Only now it has to be here and here where the battles are. He struck his forehead. His heart. Never run, boys, except straight on.

Dark now. No lines cut the sky. No marching or movement except for the scatter of clouds. Flags washed clean of all emblems and insignia and set free from poles and halyards and all restraints. I touch head, heart. My own seats of war.

The 7th — or so we hear. We look for any sign. Rebs gathering, odd orders coming down, some change in the order of things. But nothing happens except the usual. Roll call and wormy bacon. We stand around waiting for some announcement that don't come.

Oh it'll come, Gus tells us. Rebs don't usually give bacon up, worms and all. They're probably emptying the storehouse. By noon we'll know.

Noon comes. Goes.

The hour is postponed to three.

Three comes. Goes.

Then six. Then seven. All these hours come and go and not one, Marinus comments, big with blessing.

I ask Gus if he should call an evening meeting. No, he says. He's down on Willy's

India rubber pad and don't look too good.

Want me to read something to you, Gus?

Save your eyes, he tells me, then closes his.

I do an inventory of my items, which is some comfort when I'm scared. Book. Ink pen. Knife. Certificate of deposit. Pants. Shirt. Coat. Thread. Needle. Boots.

I push the certificate to one side. I look over at Gus. A spasm bends me over, then I run out with the certificate in hand. Come back with sumac berries made into a tea. Get Gus to drink.

It is typhoid fever. The red spots on Gus's neck and forearms. Marinus and I carry Gus to a group of men lying near the gate to the sick-call enclosures. Marinus bribes a guard with a certificate and we get Gus fairly close to the front, which angers some of the other sick boys. I'm sorry, I say, but he's bad off.

So're we, they shoot back.

Whenever a hospital patient is "exchanged," an orderly comes to take in a new patient. But all around us boys are dying. It will be too late for them.

At the end of the day we have to take Gus back to the tent. Least he ain't alone here, I tell Marinus. Then I say, When it comes time — For me, I mean — Gus comes up from somewhere to say I shouldn't think that way. I think how a man has to. It strikes me strange, thinking those words, as if I am a man. And yet if it means seeing clear through to something on the other side of all the color and decoration, all the acts and words, all the songs and music, then maybe I am, or at least getting close. Push it all aside like stage scenery, and there it is, so simple it scares you. I'm not afraid, I tell Marinus. I am only seeing how things are. I tell Gus he has to hang on, too. You're my boy, he says, and I say, Gus! you got to *live*.

It's not yet dark so I run to the sutlers. A few are still there, some rolling down the canvas sides to their "stores." One man unfolds a leg and looks down from his wagon seat. He's skinny everywhere except for his face, which looks swollen. What you want, boy?

Quinine, I say.

He keeps real still and talks real quiet. You don't want to say that so loud now, he tells me.

You got any?

What *you* got? he says.

I show him my items.

That's mighty poor.

It's real gold, this pen.

Lemme see.

I hand it up. He looks, hands it back. What else?

Knife. I hand it up. He looks. Says, That's only a penny or two.

Not in here, I say. In here you can sell it for a lot.

He twirls a strand of black hair. Waits still as stone.

And this coat, I say, though it makes me near ill to do so. I take needle and thread and attach them to my shirt.

Now you're getting warm, boy.

Sixty grains, I say.

A goodly amount. What else you got?

It would be sweet, I think, to walk away now. Just turn and go. I look down at my boots dusted the reddish color of ferrous sulfide. My boots, I imagine myself saying, then hear the words. There is all that now, between us. My father, Gus, the dead man at the stream. Then I stand there mute, all sound falling away. I am waiting for nothing, it seems, waiting to be waiting, waiting because there is nothing else to do.

Finally he says I'll take them things. But I can give you only a bit. Hard as bejesus to come by.

I hand up the items. He goes to his shelves. Hands down a radish and two carrots. The sight stuns me until I see, dangling among the carrots' greenery, a little glassine packet.

Walking back, I remember my tooth, there in the coat pocket. Almost go back for it.

The dirt closer now. I have to go slower. Watching where I step. And watching what's up ahead. Thus I see Willy, or someone who resembles Willy, and this person is eating what appears to be white bread. But the light is sinking, and I can't be sure. Willy! I call. He weaves me a strange course, then I give up on him, probably in one of his moods. Then I see him deep in the stream, just standing there, waving his hands about. Willy! I holler. It won't clear up this time of night. Best come out. Tomorrow you can wash. He stays there. Then I hear an infernal grunting and squealing. Some fellow off his head, crawling as fast as he can go in the muck and rushing right up to Harley. He stops, flings handfuls of mud everywhere. Harley yells at him to quit the damn screeching. The man don't quit. Harley shoots in the air, and the fellow goes berserk. I walk away, disgusted. Marinus is reading his book as if nothing in the world is happening anywhere. I administer half the quinine, only about ten grains, with well water. Sit alongside Gus. Don't want the next day. Nor today, neither.

Today Wirz spoke of our president as Mr. Lincoln. Big improvement over his usual. I think, does it mean something? Conclude that it don't.

Tonight I am on guard while the others tunnel. They will do more bickering, probably, than digging. That's how it has been these past days. Too far from here; too close to there. Soil too loose; soil too heavy. Too many well-holes already, riddling the area; not enough camouflage. The one night I tried to stick my nose into the argument, I said, more for Gus's sake, Grant's no quitter. Had all last winter to quit at Vicksburg but didn't and look where he is right now, outside Petersburg and the rebs running scared. Where'd we be if he'd a skipped? Home, somebody said. Sure, I said, and Jeff Davis king of some new country, and all the generals dukes. So what? the fellow said. Louie, spilling sand between his fingers, said Boys! This is all that's between us and freedom. It don't seem like so much, does it? That a little bit a dirt can throw a fellow. Ain't you ashamed?

Don't know if they were.

Thought leaves me. On guard outside the tent, I wake from time to time. Check the rock pile. Doze again.

Find myself washing my hands, then head,

face, and neck. I am sinking into a clear pond. It is early-morning cold. Mist rising off it. And everything so still except for the ripples I am making. Then I am drinking this water, sweet and cold. All around me are streams, rivulets, rivers, rapids, water-falls, pasture run-off, long skeins of liquid silver. I see sky-blue water, brown water, amber water, even black and pearl-gray and rose-red water, then gray with silver points and foaming white water. The sound my hand makes combing through it is a gushing deep gurgle. I dive and break a still sheet of it and there is a sudden crash of glass break-ing. I pour water in a "v" from a bucket, watch it puddling into the ground, hear the burbling racket as it strikes.

Dreaming all this, I do not hear the raiders at all. Wake to some pain foaming and swirl-ing through me. Hear moaning. It is my own. Our blankets gone, the India rubber pad. Gus bleeding along one side of his head.

They got us with our own stones.

Gus! I say, hanging onto him in the hos-pital. He wants to tell me something. About a woman. His brother's wife, I finally un-derstand. I should go there, to that farm in Bradford County. Tell her he died peacefully in camp, of an illness. I should go when they're all out haying, the men. She might be picking early apples in the orchard. There's a big orchard. The village of Neath, he says. The two of them will be a pool from which birds sip at dawn. I am to say this. Then his words jumbling. Gus, I say. I am sorry. You are worth ten of me. I mean these words as I have never meant anything before. I am holding him too hard and he says Let me go, Jim. It's time now. I want to. Pain is slashing around inside me like a thorn branch in the wind.

No quinine in this hospital. The only thing I can do for him is keep him more or less clean and put wet bandages on his forehead and make up stories about his corn and beans. Outside the tent, the day shimmers hot, a furnace of bad air, and inside here men begging for one thing or another but nobody able to give much of anything.

Marinus has traded his book for a button in order to get into this stench with me and sit with him. Seems he wants the fever himself. I do as well. Gus looks like a wet rag thrown on the earth and left there. That is how they wash patients when there is no time to do anything more. A pail of water sloshed around them. His Bible is a ruin, mostly, but we were able to find some parts not wet and falling to bits. I read to him until I get weak and light-headed. Words go black, then parts of the page, then Marinus takes the book and reads aloud. I hear her violin, the lowest and deepest parts, as he tells about vials of wrath pouring down upon the earth and the sea and the rivers and the sun and on the kingdom of the beast, while all the heat bugs are sawing away. When Marinus stops, I tell Gus Grant is winning, and that he can go if he wants to because it will be all right now, with Grant winning.

All a lie.

Then I am going, walking behind Gus who is headed for the dead line and I am so nice and quiet inside, something sinking in roots, growing and sending out leaves, I know it for death, and I think oh let him go, let him just keep going, don't let him turn and come back here. Way in the distance behind us, I hear Marinus still reading some words only they are too far away to make out. Gus becomes a sheen of light as he slips under the railing. And there ain't even any shots.

Then I'm back in the hospital tent, and an orderly is saying You boys'll have your own turn soon enough, and that's for sure.

Louie comes back and smacks me again

with his paw. Marinus pushes me out of reach. They squabble. I don't hear a thing. Orderly made us burn that Bible. Gus's face went slack at the end, Marinus said. Like dropping in battle, he said. Dropping into peace.

I am at the dead line. Go ahead! somebody says. With my compliments. But how about giving a poor fellow that shirt and those pants first? I am seeing Gus beyond the dead line and passing through the stockade walls. Soon he'll be in the pines. I start to follow. But then he has an arm around me and we're walking someplace else. Now you remember and tell her, Jim, he's saying. He points to my boots, which it seems I still have. Be like that, he's saying. I am so pleased to find him still alive, I turn and grab him around the shoulders. Am I ever glad to see you, Gus! He nods, then frees himself, and starts moving off. I go to follow but he turns around and his face becomes strange, frowning and mean-like.

Yet I am awash with some ferocious joy. It was him, I think. It was Gus.

I step back away from the dead line, knowing he would want me to.

When I come into my own skin again, I see that it is Marinus who has me clutched around the shoulders and we are making our way back to our spot.

It is wrenching to me that he did not know my true name.

Marinus, I say later. Why didn't you let me go? Follow your philosophy and just let me be?

He says something about a foolish consistency.

I sleep and wake and then it crawls over me again, the knowing that he is gone, but more than that, that death is here, that I am it, a knowing that sinks into the skin and through it, and down through what is left of the muscles and it finds bone and sinks into that and spreads itself all through me, bones to blood to nerves to brain and I am old, so old with it, I feel ancient and eternal with knowing, a stone in the deeps of the earth.

Seven

Thought you died on me, boy, Sergeant Moore says. I say no, had to tend to some things. He puts me back in the fever section and it is good. I have whiskey before, during, and after. The first swallow is like eating fire. The second, a cooler fire. The third numbs the edges of me so I'm not seeing Gus in the form of each fellow lying there in his pool of bloody flux. Outside, the day burns hot. Inside, a sour mess, everybody begging for something. There is a bucket for soaking cloths and another for wastes and a third for washing the patients. On a low stool, our bottles of tonic from poplar bark. In a cabinet, the whiskey. I steal the patients' rations sometimes. I don't report deaths right away and winnow out another ration or two. I look down the rows of sick and dying men and the rows burn away into light. *If the arrow of prayer*, I read to the boys, *is to enter heaven, it has to come from a soul full-bent.* The words swim, little fishes.

Hear myself saying Let the sinews of my soul burn with belief, but it is so much raving of the brain.

And now hollering on the outside. In the

pen. And I too numb and brain-blind to even think what it might mean.

After it all dies down, Sergeant Moore comes over to me. Looks me in the eye. Boy, he says. Best go back. You're fairly pickled.

In the pen I hear Wirz has shot everybody — using blanks. To learn 'em a lesson. Was to be a big break-out, Wirz heard. We all know it for humbug, but he says if such a thing is attempted, he will fire on us as long as there is a man left kicking.

When the numbness wears off, leaving a ruffle of pain, I say Louie, I'm going with you. Marinus gives me a look but keeps his words to himself.

I run with Louie and his boys — much as it can be called running. It is good work, rounding them up. Not letting a one slip away. It helps almost as good as the whiskey.

And Louie, too, gets us whiskey. Don't know where it comes from. Don't care. Just want the fire of it to scour away at the brain and then I am all right for a time. Can sleep.

I have never witnessed a hanging. When there was one in Montrose, the gallows erected between the jail and the courthouse, my mother forbade me to go. Later, boys told me about it, proud as anything.

Marinus will not attend this one. Anything for a diversion, he says, and the more gruesome the better. Louie says he shouldn't get high-toned. He ain't done a thing to help and yet he yaps at those who do. I feel somewhat bad and edgy, siding with Louie.

With a file he gave me, I am sawing away at his beard. He is a dignitary now, head of the pen's vigilance committee. With my needle and blue thread I have sewn up his blouse. Today the committee and the "Regulators" are to have the honor of receiving the tried and convicted raiders at half-past four. Willy is cleaning Louie's boots with a bandage bloodied on only one side.

Louie wants to know how he looks. Good we say. The King of France.

There's a crowd around the six-man gallows. Louie pushes through to the front. The side gate opens. There's Wirz, on his bay, followed by six raiders under heavy guard. The leader of the raiders, a red-headed man named Collins, is first.

Wirz's face is still as a shovel. These men, he says, have been tried and found guilty, and I now deliver them to you in as good a condition as I received them. Do with them what justice, reason, and mercy dictate. And may God protect both you and them.

Nice words, I think, for such a son of Satan.

The men climb the scaffold, which is planks laid over barrels. Wirz turns his horse, but then there is Father Blaze, grabbing at the bridle.

Wirz dismounts, and we all try to see. But they go around behind the bay. Then the priest goes up to the condemned men. Wirz leaves.

We wait, but nothing more happens except the priest goes from one raider to the next, talking a while and taking his time.

The crowd all around starts heaving forward a little, hollering at the priest. Our turn now!

He takes no notice. Finally he raises his arm in blessing, but one of the raiders hollers out Talk to the Regulators for us! A confusion ensues, and one fellow up on the scaffold comes bounding down and with friends grouping around him, he makes it through the guards and gets all the way to the sinks before getting caught and hauled back.

I knew he would, so I haven't moved. There is no stopping the thing that has started. It will be done.

He's bellowing but four of the others are twisting and kicking against the sides of the barrels. The fifth, Collins, lies on the ground, his rope broken.

Friends! the captured raider calls out. I'm innocent. Then he's hanging too, but holding onto the rope, trying to break the fall. He goes limp and I have to look away.

A Regulator stands up on the platform, alongside the hanging men. Any new boys here, he says, take a good look at the penalty for thievin'!

When I get back, Marinus asks what I learnt.

Don't know for sure, I say.

Chinese boxes, he says. Little punishments inside bigger ones.

Ain't order important? I ask him.

Some say so.

I don't tell him what I think in my heart. That maybe we hanged an innocent man. It's true some newcomers bury their things under their tents. Might not have been stolen goods at all. The fellow looked like a storekeeper, big rounded face. Just the kind to squirrel items away for safekeeping.

So now I sit here staring at the ashen sticks of our cook fire but am seeing the gallows again, then the pile of men I hit with the wagon spoke. It is all there, in the smallest of boxes, and myself too.

Tell me what I was supposed to learn, I say to Marinus.

He looks up. Did we do right, he says. Right. Right to the country where we came from.

Must get some half-decent food or else I am going to tumble into the mud like some waterlogged tree.

Ain't it a sad thing, Harley says to me today, to think how all this wouldn't be if you all didn't come down here an' raise a fight.

You're the ones, I say. You wanted the fight. You fired first.

There's another fellow crawling around, heaving mud about. Or maybe it's the same one as before. Why not just go ahead and shoot him, I say, if it's all our fault. Look at him trying to escape!

Mad at me, Harley fires over the fellow's head. If he wasn't gone off his brain before, he surely is now.

Men are leaving the spot, trying to get out of the way. I push at Harley's gun and he swings it around, knocking me down easily, and there I am, with the crazy man in the mud.

We are hearing trains coming and going. What does it mean? We hear a gust of distant cheering. What does it mean? We are as

125

attuned as creatures to hints from the outer world. What does such and such *mean?* We are sick for meaning at times. Rage for it. A new fellow attached to our "ninety" speculates that the rebs probably just heard the news that the Federal skirmish line is now only three miles outside of Atlanta.

Now soldiers mounting the scaffolding, lining up near the Florida Artillery up there, and looking out toward the woods. What does it mean?

They say they will put us between themselves and any advancing enemy. Sounds of protest and disgust come from all over the pen as this new rumor draws blood.

We hear trees splintering and crashing. What does it mean? Work details making breastworks?

We take it all seriously, then don't, for what does it mean finally?

I eye Gus's tasseling corn and flowering beans. I see myself running somewhere with them, the corn a kind of flag of my own.

The rebs come down off the scaffolding. What does it mean?

Sign right here, Louie is telling me, holding out a pencil and a piece of paper on a board.

I stare at the scribbles. What does it mean? I say.

Just sign, dammit.

What is it?

Petition. Sign.

Petition?

To the president and the governors.

Which president?

Jim, he says, you gone crazy? There's but one true one.

What do we want him to do?

Just sign. You're holding up the show.

I creep through the scrawly words . . . *The Undersigned . . . Demand Release by Parole or Exchange . . .*

What the hell's the matter with you boy? Sign the dang thing.

I am struck dumb by thought. A petition goes against the grain of things. If we have not been paroled up to now, the president and governors probably don't want us to be for reasons only they know. A petition means that the one asked for something has the power to grant it, and if he don't, it must mean it's because he don't want to. So if we sign, it is a kind of disloyalty. We want what they think ain't best. On the other hand, signing is a way of being a footprint. Is prayer, I wonder, a treasonous act? Or is it being a footprint? Caught in the thicket of all this, I believe I have suddenly become Marinus.

Louie thumps me on the back. What you waitin' for? Judgment Day?

I sign. *Ira Cahill Stevens.* Look at the words which seem to mean nothing.

Tonight, Louie says.

I start digging up the corn.

You gone crazy? Louie says.

Taking them along, I say.

No you ain't, he says. You can't take them through.

Can.

Those damn leaves'll make too much noise.

No they won't.

Said you can't. Stick 'em back in that dirt, Jim.

Name ain't Jim.

It ain't? Thought it was.

Ain't. It's Ira.

Ira! All right. Stick 'em back in that dirt.

No.

I have the corn out. Am wrapping the roots in my shirt. Louie heaves himself at me. I dodge away. Ira! Give 'em to me.

I laugh. Squabbling over a damn corn-stalk. The leaves rustle overhead like petticoats rattling and swishing. We dodge each other, Louie turning the air blue with his cussing.

Then he just lays down and looks at the sky. I go over to him. What? I say. He grabs for the corn. I skitter back.

We are gone crazy for sure.

The tunnel is holding. It is taking them a long time to get mealbags out. And the night breezy and dark. So it seems we are going to go, all of us. And the corn. Then I am seeing small lights. Firebugs, I think, but they come closer. Get bigger.

Five rebs with muskets. Lanterns.

Come up outa there, you sons a bitches.

Willy appears. Then another fellow. Then Louie. The rebs jeer at Mr. Law and Order. Mr. Committee Man. A reb slithers down into the tunnel, comes out, says they are going to commission Louie in the CSA and put him in charge of tunnels. Either that or shoot him then and there. What's your pick, boy?

Louie's a stone.

All that diggin' must make you all good and hungry now. That true?

Louie's still a stone.

Tell you what, the reb says. Fill it in yerselves and get double rations tomorrow. If we do it, it's the Captain's necklace for you all.

We know what this means. They stretch

a fellow head to foot between two planks. The upper one is raised notch by notch until the fellow faints. Sometimes dies.

Louie nods.

Passing Willy, one of the rebs says Nice work, boy.

Louie hears this. Gives Willy a look.

Then we are working hard. Lifting and passing on, getting rid of and getting some more to get rid of, the sky lightening in the east and staying that way for a long while, the morning being born in its own good time, and the walls rebuilding themselves in the long slow coming of light.

The rebs are dozing. The camp is waking up. Nobody gets too close to us, everybody knowing. Louie himself tamps down the dirt. I carry the corn back. Stick it into the earth. Tamp it down.

At roll call Willy is absent and this causes a pack of trouble. Delayed rations being only one part of it. Then there's Willy, but he don't stay. In the next minute he's running toward the stream. I go after him, hear a shot. Willy's in the water, running away from Harley. I get into the water and grab Willy and try to drag him out with me, but there's Louie, looking down at us, waiting. Willy gets away from me and runs straight at Harley who fires and don't miss.

★ ★ ★

Sunset now. The sky to the west all striped and glowy. Board wall every which way I look. But beyond the south wall, Florida and the Gulf of Mexico. And to the east, beyond wall, sentry boxes, pines, the Atlantic Ocean. The thing is to keep clear on all this. Hold it fast.

As I am holding two pieces of corn pone soggy with molasses. Then I'm chewing. Not wanting to swallow. Needing it to last.

Louie has grabbed our last blanket off the poles. It is for Willy's burial.

Blanket will get stolen but Louie don't care. He carried Willy out of the stream himself.

Was it him? I asked.

Louie just gave me a nothing look and walked off.

You coming back?

Don't believe so.

Where you going?

Don't know.

He has seceded.

Now I am trying to think what to do. Thought circling like turkey buzzards, pairs and pairs of 'em, wings outstretched, black and white. When I close my eyes they alight, hopping down, folding their wings, and stride right over to where I lay.

And I know what it means.

Jerk awake. Think how in the woods creatures hear gusts of wind and somehow know "storm." But they don't pen one another up. Factions of rabbits don't wage war on other rabbits. Buzzards neither. It is no darn good being a reasoning creature. I resolve never to reason any more. I am through for good with all of that. Will be a rabbit. A buzzard. I sleep. Head under arm, buzzard-like.

Eight

Bleating ayes and booming nays. What happened to the petition? They want our ayes, the rebs. Want Mr. Lincoln to do what ain't in him to do. Bleats outnaying nays.

New boys coming in by the hundreds. Gate of hell wide open &ct. Most "hundred day" men come in with belongings. They were caught by Early in his Pennsylvania raid. Cavalry boys from Sherman's outfit, though, robbed of nearly every shred. One fellow walking proudly by, not worried about where he's stepping but maybe thinking he is still on his horse. What's the news? I call. He stops as if about to pass the time of day. Don't seem to mind that his shoulders and back are raw-red and blistered. Your furlough, sir, will be over in two weeks, he says. There's to be an exchange in August.

They tell you that?

It's in the papers, he says.

Everybody? I say.

That I don't know.

Then he proceeds on his procession. The knife of hope still in him.

I believe him. I don't believe him. I go to the central gate to watch more come in, hundreds more, the bunch of us pressing in close just to see. The rebs fire overhead. Too close! they holler. Yer too damn close! Think we want to rush the gate but we don't. Just want to see all that Federal blue. The great blue parade of it. This beggar not blind!

They are busy busy busy. Cutting trees, surging through the camp looking for volunteers on their big guns, wanting us to train their boys, and now they're putting up little white flags showing where we can't go, near the central gate.

I am in a mood for talk, why I don't know, but Marinus ain't talking much these days and so I say to a reb, I would not be a slave so I would not be a master. Know who said that?

One of your nigger-lovers probably. Git back.

I say Benjamin Franklin. It's in my book.

He says I don't care if it was Moses himself. Git back!

Wandering about, I spy Louie building a stove for some new boys. They still have something. Straps, boots, forms. I creep close to Louie. Let me help you. Don't want help.

Louie —

Best go, Jim. Don't wanta thump you.

Name's Ira.

Don't care what it is. Git.

I go back to our spot and water the withering corn and beans.

Tonight a reb chaplain climbs a little stage. Holds up an issue of the *New York Herald*. Reads Immediate exchange probable. New boys whoop and holler. We don't. Hymn-singing rises.

What's the day? I ask a new boy.

Thursday, he says.

What's the month?

August.

Thursday. August. Words right there but hard to reach. Shiny stones glittering too deep underwater. Thank you I say and he drifts elsewhere.

Watermelon and pie.

What kind?

Rhubarb.

Strawberry.

Blackberry.

Hayfoot.

Strawfoot.

Peas'n ham.

Chicken'n dumplings.

Bread'n butter.

Knives'n forks.

Sugar'n cream.

Cream'n coffee.
Cakes'n cream.
What kind?
Peach.
Charlotte Russe.
Who's she?
It's a dessert.
Granddaddy porcupine.
Who's he?
He's a dessert, too.
Ain't!
Is so.
How d'you make it?
With everything.
*Every*thing?
Anything sweet you want to put in, you put in.

Coconuts?
Coconuts.
Cream?
Cream.
We'll be epiphytes, taking sustenance from airy words.

What kind of feet?
Mosses, orchids, lichens. Live on air.
Might have a chance then, you think?
Gave up thought.
How we talk, Marinus and I.
You suppose, I ask, it's because they haven't made up their minds yet about their flag and

so have all these little white ones to dote on? Color in later, maybe?

How many you say they moved?

Twenty closer by two feet to the wall. Twenty-eight farther out by three feet.

Clear as day then.

What.

You don't see it?

No, I don't.

That they have some plan, boy. Now. Strawberries.

Didn't we say that already?

Not strawberries'n cream.

Cream, then.

Thunder growls to the northwest. Shots in direction of east wall. The first drops of rain hit.

Marinus? They say those fifteen were truly exchanged.

But also, I'm thinking, frames for barracks dragged in. And men all over the camp calling for indignation meetings.

Try as I might, can't stop reasoning.

Heard that too, he says.

Why only fifteen?

Put out the mush-tin.

Who wins the battle, Marinus?

Hayfoot.

Strawfoot.

How we talk, in the rain.

★ ★ ★

Thunderstorms. Lions growling overhead, one after another. But rebs working through it all, fixing their little white flags. I believe I am dreaming it, so much fussing with those infernal flags.

Why you keeping on with them? I ask one of the rebs.

Orders.

But why?

Can't say.

Don't you know why they want 'em just so?

Don't know.

Or you can't say.

Both. Either. Whichever one you want. Now git back.

Flap, flap, flap they go, on a day green and murky as pond water. I try to trot away. Can't. Muscles drying up sore and stiff as soaked leather.

Storms and showers, showers and storms. And a big storm wind gusting through the camp dousing fires and the sky sliding into purple and every creature within this pen edgy with it. Louie appears. Flash flood! he hollers at us. Wager anybody fifty dollars, payable after we're out of here. Look at that sky! Walls going to go! I follow him to the east side. He shows me the cut-out sluice opening for the stream. There'll be a jam-up there, the whole damn thing's going to go.

Louie is back, I think, and hope blows through me like that storm wind.

You just run, he says.

It commences with a hard smoky rain. We cheer the gash lighting. The fireball lightning. Rain comes like shot in mid-day night. Louie is yelling, taking charge. He motions toward the stream. It's high and brown, foaming, pulling down chunks of bank into it, riling it all away. Boards are bobbing down.

Let's go! Louie yells, and we run, Marinus and I.

He is right. Boards from the west walls are hurtling downstream, but prisoners are jumping into the stream, trying to retrieve them. Some boys get swung around in the rapid water and holler for help. More boards come pouring down and prisoners dive for them. I see that little black dog paddling, then tell myself No! Can't be. Then I don't see it at all.

Freedom, you jackasses, Louie is yelling. Freedom not firewood! Advance! Advance! Rush the damn walls.

Some of us do. Big guns are booming. And the east wall is swaying like a piece of paper. We've already trampled through the dead line. If shot is coming at us, we don't hear it. And still some of us boys are going after those boards. Louie a madman. The walls! he screams. Charge the walls!

It topples, falling outward, posts giving way in the waterlogged earth. I press against men in front of me, the mass of us nearly horizontal. Then we're flowing over that wall only to see a line of rebs in battle formation waiting for us, guns level, then firing. I feel the tide shift and I'm sucked back in on the panicky rush.

Tonight the central gates open to admit three hundred boys from Sherman's army. They march in between those white flags. Rebs still working in the mist to close up the gap in the wall.

Nature and war, Marinus says, lay all things prostrate but the rebs.

This can't be, I say.

Is, he says.

I look at him straight on. We can give up or we can go on, what d'you want to do?

The one eye winks a little. Might get better, he says.

What? This?

The entertainment.

Then you want to stick?

Can't get a whole lot worse.

Well, it can. I'm thinking of O'Ryan, our

mess sergeant. The scurvy settling in his ankles and feet, putrefying holes showing up, wide enough to poke a finger in. I'm also thinking of Gus. He has just come to mind.

All right then, I say. We'll stick. But only for a little while longer. I am getting plain sick of this whole show.

But the truth is, it's almost humorous. And we both know it.

Soaked earth sends up a humid haze. Not one breeze. Mosquitoes so big you can saddle and bridle 'em. This earth looks like old blood. Marinus don't believe in Him. He don't believe in hell either. It is inside us, he told me today. It is a lack.

Like hunger, I said? Or like not being free?

More in what we choose to see, or not. Choose to do, or not.

This is Hell, I said, or pretty near, and we didn't make it.

Oh no? he said.

You use niggers in your army, the reb Officer of the Day says to those of us standing behind the white flags.

Well you use dogs, one of us says back.

Only here we do.

No, sir. Richmond. Florence. Everywhere, damn near.

Ain't as bad as using niggers.

You do that too! Who's cuttin' your firewood? Who's cookin' your food?

Ain't the same.

Boys from Sherman's army tell us Atlanta's more than half gone. Atlanta's falling, burning right to the ground. One of them waves a Macon newspaper and shouts, Mobile fort surrendered without a shot!

Hooing and hollering.

These boys are rowdy, dirty, missing all their gear and most of their clothing. But they march in like heroes, and the batch of us cheering to the sky.

More news now. That Macon paper says exchanges to commence August 15th and somebody says it's the 10th today.

Marinus rebuffing all overtures to discourse.

I am afraid to say this but I am hopeful again, the knife doing its work. How much better off would we be if we could learn not to hope? Or would we be dead?

I meander through the camp, view the wreckage everywhere, then come upon Louie building another stove for somebody. Mosquitoes are bad and he slaps at them, then puffs over the work. He has lost his roundness, is now a string like the rest of us. I tell him about Atlanta but he has already heard. I ask him about the 15th, what he thinks.

He lifts a handful of mud. Says he believes in that and that alone. I tell him he sounds like Marinus. He says The fellow still alive? Give him my regards. He sits back, looks toward the sentry post nearest us. Then points. I see photographers setting up their apparatus. Louie says They're aiming to fix us here forever is what I think.

One of the new Plymouth prisoners comes out of his sturdy blanket tent, says to Louie He your helper? Louie nods and the fellow says to me Here, boy. Hands me something shiny.

Silver dollar.

I scrape it against bones, wanting to believe in it. The day so strange and the light a pearl and soon maybe it just might crack open and there we'll be, in some new world.

Here is how it goes in here. We learn there's to be a notice posted at mid-day and be clear on it, it is going to tell of exchanges. It focuses our attention. We burn. Everything we look upon seems important. Every little thing any reb does, we try to interpret. Marinus and I are eating carrots purchased with my dollar. We are eating carrots and considering the merits — Marinus's rhyme — of the notice that is soon to be posted. We scan the camp, as Marinus puts it, for details radiant with meaning.

Mid-day comes. Up goes the notice right on schedule. We rush to see it for ourselves, but even before we get there we hear the roars of disgust.

Immediate exchange probable.

The same thing that reb chaplain said a while back. Marinus says They take away today but give us tomorrow. Then he laughs.

Then more news. The *Macon Telegraph* is saying General Grant has replaced General Hunter with General Sheridan. But Grant's campaign is a failure.

Why are they saying that? I ask. You suppose he's retreating from Petersburg? How can it be? — an absolute failure.

Easy enough, says Marinus.

Boys around us get letters from time to time. This is hard to fathom. How letters find us here, but they seem to. We look at them longingly. It seems a shocking wealth. And how they absorb themselves in these letters. It is as if those boys reading their letters have ten times more life than we do. A hundred times. It seems as if they belong to a different race of beings and we will never get there in a hundred years.

The sight of a piece of paper in a fellow's hands, to me, hurts more than hope itself.

So I have made up my own letter. Goes like this. My dear Ira, Your mother came to the shop with word about your situation and I was heartily sorry to hear of it, you can be sure. Here in town both the *Democrat* and the *Independent-Republican* are railing against the whole shameful business. I figure the hold-up is due to politics, a damn sour mess if ever there was one. Man can talk his head off, give fifty good reasons for something, but politics all comes down to fellows wanting power plain and simple, and once they get it, doing what they wanted to do all along and now can, legally. The good citizens of the town are now holding indignation meetings over at the courthouse, expressing strong opinions and reeling off arguments by the yard. What this might avail you finally, I can't say, my boy, but I am in hopes you'll find immediate practical use for the enclosed.

And I find a packet of quinine. Sixty grains, at least.

Now I must tell you, he goes on, that the Bonhoffer young lady was here, inquiring after you. You know the one I mean, the one that plays the fiddle. I was sorry to be the bearer of bad news. She seemed to take it hard. She's a pretty enough lass but aims to run herself sick and done up with so much needless schooling and fiddling. Somebody should talk some sense into her if that mother and father of hers ain't capable of it.

And now speaking of that father, I know you done what you figured was right, Ira. And I know how that fellow can talk, weave a person around. He is known for it, though you could not have known it. They will be holding his trial soon and then we will see. It is another sour mess. But I am writing to say I have forgiven you. And had it been any other fellow but Bonhoffer, a legitimate scheme, say, I might not have been adverse myself.

I stop here. Go on after awhile. He tells me things are at sixes and sevens in the shop. A new lad makes mistakes and he has to spend hours each night mousing them out. He tells me not to go begging for trouble as he is hoping to have me back there soon. Until then, he remains my friend, J. L. Casey.

I see his cranky cramped penmanship. See the five dollars in greenbacks he has wrapped in an editorial from the *Independent-Republican*. Each sentence of his is a place to visit.

Each casts up a world of things. The black prescription case, the best St. Louis had to offer my grandfather. The red show globes. The oak bins and shelves. And I see her, asking about me.

I tell Marinus about the money, say I'm going to go get sumac berries. He tells me not to waste my money on him. I tell him Vegetables too. We squabble a while.

It passes the time.

Then he says Son, sweet poison for our thirst, hope.

He turns to a fellow sitting dazed in the dirt. Sir, he says, you argue that the highest end of government is the culture of men. I ask How so? Ain't it the waging of war? And if the waging of war, then all this must follow as necessity, as right and true and good. But if the culture of men, what is this, sir? Kindly enlighten us. We humbly await your views.

Pleased to make your acquaintance, he says.

It's true, Marinus goes on, those words of the sage. *We think our civilization is near the meridian but we are only at the cock crowing and morning star.*

Yes, indeed, the fellow replies.

Deepest night well before the dawn, the well of night, sir, the deepest well of night.

Look for yourself. What do you see if not that?

A damn mess.

Marinus holds up a letter only he can see. Before this letter, sir, he says, I feel helpless. It may tell me this or it may tell me that. Good or bad, I cannot change what I'll find in here, sir. But helplessness is a great thing. Shows us where we are. Strips away illusion, cuts us down to size. Whittles away, whittles away until we see ourselves for the splinters we are. Splinters with all sorts of need and ambition. Imagine that, sir. An ambitious splinter!

You got somethin' there.

From Maximus, Marinus says, I learned self-government, and not to be led aside by anything, and cheerfulness in all circumstances —

Sounds like a good idea, the man says.

We sit there. I am thinking of the way she plays her fiddle. The way she looks at nothing, playing. Or maybe she is seeing beyond everything into the nothing of it all. Maybe she climbs down all those little notes straight into it and looks right at it, the face of time maybe, the real face of all this that is.

Flap, flap, flap, they go, the little flags.

White in moonlight, white in sunlight, white in rain. Grave-marker flags. Surrender flags. Gravely we wait behind them.

Nine

It is August 20th — near as anyone can figure. We hear Captain Wirz is sick. The hangman and torturer, the withholder of rations, of news, of sanitation, of medicines, is sick and sick bad, the very color of death. He is in Macon. Sick and apt to die. Hurrah, boys! Hurrah for the Union! Hooray for God and country! Wirz, damn him to hell, is dying, hallelujah! and we are going to get sweet potatoes now. Be gaggin' on 'em bad as on the cornmush soon, so they tell us, but pass 'em on anyhow! Wirz sick and maybe gone before long. Bury him deep, boys! Sweet potatoes on the way, hurrah!

This is what we are saying.

And even more to strum about. Rebs asking for a thirty-day armistice, wanting to talk peace and Mr. Lincoln granting it.

So we hear.

Marinus says If so he was duped. Want a rest is all.

I try to gather thoughts blown about and spinning. But if Grant failed, I say, why an armistice? It don't make sense.

Ira, he says, you know what? You have grown wise. This place does a wonder for you!

We are clean. We are clean and wearing clothes washed in the stream and dried on spiny reeds. Our stomachs ain't giving us the devil for they are full of beef and bacon and beans and corn pone and molasses.

All this in honor of our new camp commander's inauguration. Lieutenant S. B. Davis.

Marinus and I stroll about. Come upon a group near the white flag parade route. Our boys listening to two reb officers, one of them fancied up in unsullied buckskin hat, patent leather boots, tailored gray uniform, a vision of a fellow.

What's Jeff Davis up to? one of our boys asks these two.

Hidin' from Sherman! comes the answer from the batch of us.

Somebody else yells Tryin' to get Egypt camels through the blockade!

The fancy fellow lofts out his voice. President Davis, he says, regrets the suffering resulting from this war. I assure you he deeply regrets the suffering and loss of life on both sides. But you all can see, can you not, the necessity for it? We are just being true to the principles of our Revolutionary Fathers. A government receives its power from the consent of the people, and since

151

we have not consented to losing our rights as states, we are free to establish our own government. It was a tyranny of numbers, what happened to the South. She had to act. Y'all would have done the same.

Marinus wipes sweat from his face. He fixes his shirt. Sir, he calls, stunning me. The crowd around us shifts, opening up, everybody gawking at us.

Speak, the fancy fellow says.

In the hard quiet Marinus says, Do you believe that all men are created equal?

I understand the direction of your question, the officer says. But I believe that states can legislate for themselves on matters of slavery.

On the basis of what right?

From the consent of the governed, sir.

All of the governed?

All those that can vote.

Marinus has to take a deep breath. He sways a little, closing his eyes. I go to pull him away but the fancy fellow says Let him talk. Marinus gets hold of himself and says Well that sounds like the tyranny of — He starts coughing. The fancy fellow lowers his head and looks at his boots. Marinus's voice is dry and croaky but he gets out An unbridled . . . majority. Ain't that what your president calls it?

Hoo! shouts some of the boys.

The fellow says I assure you we have a constitution.

Why d'you even need one? Marinus counters. If states have sovereignty. Sounds like a contradiction.

We don't believe it is, sir.

But the officer's face is getting pinker. The fellow with him is puckering his mouth up as if to spit.

Belief, Marinus says. Always a big help, hey? What happened to your other one?

Which do you refer to?

Your other constitution. Of the United States.

Null and void. Don't bind us a bit.

Then allow me to suggest — That you don't exist, sir.

The two officers laugh.

How so, sir?

Marinus holds up his right arm. Cut this off, does it belong to your body anymore?

No, sir.

Can it act on its own?

No, it cannot.

States that cut themselves off from the body of the United States have no power whatsoever. You are nothing, sir. You don't . . . exist. Besides, you're a traitor and a criminal.

We all go quiet and scared now.

If I exist at all, you mean!

The fancy fellow is smiling, walking off.

I get Marinus away from the crowd and help him lay down. Marinus says That was a good parting shot.

Is it true, I say, that the state of Georgia don't really exist, nor any of the others?

It's just . . . words.

But it makes sense.

That's the trouble with words.

He's sinking away. Marinus, I say, to pull him back, you were grand. It's true.

You liked that? You don't exist and therefore all slaves are in fact free men . . . That's logic for you. Always a treat.

I feel for his pulse. Marinus, I could not have done it, I say. I am proud just — Knowing you.

Don't be, he says.

Are you sinking on me?

Tired, he says. Just —

I let him sleep. I sit there on guard, receiving congratulations from the boys. They tell me that the dandy officer was none other than S. B. Davis himself.

Which is why they all were such scared rabbits.

Lieut. Davis has issued us shovels for latrines and we are ordered to use them for such. Louie in the clouds over this, but boys don't want to take any chances now. Everybody thinking Exchange. But can we last is the question. At roll call thirty-six of our ninety couldn't stand. Marinus going lame too. I have charge of the sick boys in our mess and get their rations for them. It may be possible to last if Lieut. Davis stays on. Otherwise, no. Then we are all dead men.

Gums bleeding. Scurvy. Have given up looking for wagon-loads of sweet potatoes. For a full day, each hour, I willed wagons of them to enter the camp, but if there are such potatoes anywhere in this country, they are not entering this camp. Fear my teeth will all fall out now. Orderly has given me a tablespoon of sumac berries for tea. I heat water, drink the bitter tea. I can see it, that territory where you give up and become someone else, surrendering. It is right over there, in the haze, waiting for me. I hear it calling my old name. Jim! Jim!

No — it's Louie, drunk, trying to hang onto a shovel. He pitches forward but don't let go of it.

Look what — he's saying. Look what — The crazy fool —

He starts laughing. Then he's crying. Laughing and crying and saying *latrines* over and over. He is wringing himself out, holding the issued shovel tight against his chest.

Wirz is back. Rations cut. And we are to surrender all shovels. Louie says he has buried his. He's waiting, he says, for the right crew. Don't want us. Now he is working at the burial grounds. Gets whiskey there. I am in a funk over all this. What to do? I read my book to Marinus. Seems a fool thing to do, but there is no frigate like a book, after all. Do you know what bad habits are? They are the thistles of the heart. Each indulgence in them is a seed from which will spring a new crop of weeds. And do you know that an ill-favored snake is a better companion than a well-favored harlot, for a harlot is the Eve of a serpent. I read Marinus this. It gets him to smile, at least. Then he recites me something that says if you work at what is right in front of you and use your reason and don't get distracted, and if you keep your divine part, whatever that is, pure as if you had to give it back anytime soon, and if you hold well to all of the above, and not expect things or fear things, and if you are satisfied with whatever it is you are now doing, supposing it is in tune with nature and such and you're not a liar, you're going to live happy, and there won't be any man

156

who can prevent it.

After a pause he says But we have out-grown Marcus Aurelius, haven't we? Seems we need some new words.

How about these? I say. *Abundant sleep is essential to bodily efficiency and to that alertness of mind which is all-important in an engagement; and few things more certainly and more effectually prevent sound sleep than eating heartily after sundown, especially after a heavy march or desperate battle.*

We look at one another, and he says Those'll do just dandy. Then we look out at the day again and where we are in it.

Louie off his head. Comes here to badger us. It is the whiskey. Calls me a traitor and a spy. Then accuses Marinus. He staggers and falls and we go help him and he rails at us. All of us sinking like weakened swimmers in this infernal heat and not-knowing. Marinus now sleeping most of the day, or trying to, face hidden from the sun. I sit here, on guard. It is something and not nothing. He has gotten a new book somehow, and while he sleeps I look at it. *Woodbury's Shorter Course in German Grammar.* Today I am reading the lessons on weak declensions, whatever those are. When I push out of them thickets, I wake Marinus and go get the sick boys' rations. If anyone has died, I take the extras for us. It would help, Marinus tells me over our dinner, if we could know for sure that malice don't reach beyond the grave.

He has diarrhea bad. Internal abcess?
Just don't bleed, I tell him. Say to yourself, I will not.
Son — he says, going weak on me.
They're saying the 6th, Marinus. The 6th. You hear me? Exchanges for real.
Boom, he says. And I say it back. Meaning their rumors and our gullibility are fighting it out on the line.
You just hang on now, I say. I give him water stolen from our former well. Have to sneak back there with our mush-tin. Louie surprised me one day while I was there. Grabbed me by the shoulders. Jim, he said.
His bony face all light.
Say you are, he said.
Say I am what?
With me. Are you?
Why, Louie?
I got a plan.
I'm with Marinus and we —
Leave him! He's dying. Besides, what's he good for? Talk is all. If you stick with him, he'll drag you down too. He's a dead man. You know that!

What about the 6th, Louie? Look at that hillside. It's half-empty. They're maybe starting already.

Believe that, you're lunier than me. They're dying is all.

How come you know everything all the time?

I know because they're laughing at it at the burial pit. At the dead-house. I listen! I know! My plan's a good one. Just the two of us. Needs us two is all. I can do it on my own but two is better.

You said I was a traitor and a spy, Louie.

Didn't mean it. Just raving. You with me?

You go. You just go and I hope you —

He pelts me and I go teetering.

I can't run, I say. I can't —

What's the matter with you? Your legs?

No. Not my legs. Well, yes, but this too, I say, hitting my forehead. And this. My chest.

We stand there a while, each of us locked still and staring at one another.

Go with strength, I tell myself. Go with the strength that's left. But I don't.

I wake up by the stream, Harley nearby with his rifle. I dreamed I put Marinus in the water, it was so clear and moving nice, taking us right to the sluice and there was Louie with a shovel.

I tell this dream to Harley. You're luny, he says.

What about you?

What d'you think?

I don't tell him what I think. What good would it do?

I go back to Marinus.

Wisdom is the olive, I read to him, *which springs from the heart, blooms on the tongue, and bears fruit in the actions.*

Makes him laugh a little, as I hoped.

Rain-smells inside this furnace of heat. The light glowing over all of us, then sinking to a kind of purple. I'm asking you again, Marinus says. Don't mean to sound cowardly, but my work is done. I've paid in full.

Don't talk foolish.

Son, do what you're most afraid of doing, always.

Well that means I probably have to live, then.

Hard to believe, but I have bested him — for the time being. Then he says a while later Son, to ask you again, might seem whiney, but I have to do it.

Wants me to kill him. How can I do that?

Patrick Evert, who has taken over my job of getting the boys' rations, is supposed to bring ours. So far he has not. On top of it all my belly is raw with hunger.

Son, he says, let me go.

He's bleeding again.

If you want to go, I say, seeing that blood seeping all around him, you have to go on your own without any permission from me.

I don't mean to sound so mad. Rain comes down. A gush. It rinses away the blood. I can't bear to see him lying there in it, face right to it, his book getting ruined. I put it under my shirt, with mine. I go over to Harley and give him a push from behind, scaring him. Shoot me, I say. You got to. Look at me trying to escape. Shoot me, then go over there and shoot him. You can have these two books, if you do.

You're crazy. Git away.

Harley —

I can't!

You got to. I am attacking you. See? I fall against him. He splashes away through the mud, making slow progress.

Harley! I call.

Morning. He is dead. I'm sure of it. Everywhere I look, small lakes, and all those around Marinus tinted red.

There is nothing on the far hillside. Just rubble. No cook fires. Nobody moving.

I sit here envious of a dead man and don't know what to do with myself.

161

Loneliness has come to pitch its camp inside me. His. Finding its new home.

I pray to the Lord to send his train to take me home. Then I'm swimming and water becomes watery air, green-tinted. I look down through this water and see two rags, mud brown. Makes me sorry, then not. Then I'm floating upward through silvery air and it is so agreeable to be inside this light that I smile. But then I make a mistake. I look back down at those rags. See one of them move. The one once belonging to Marinus flops an arm over the one once belonging to me. I sink through the watery air. Down, down, down, and when I open my eyes, there is Marinus's arm on my chest. A weight.

Not dead yet? he says.

Still here, I say. Me too.

We were yesterday here, he says. Shall today here be.

Patrick Evert comes with our rations. You boys look pretty down, he says.

Are, I say.

A while later, or maybe it is the next day, Sam'l Fletcher comes by to pray with us. We don't want his prayer. Want his corn pone which he don't give up.

Harley wanders past, slows, keeps going.

I wonder if he has taken a furlough after shooting Willy. Taken a furlough, then come back in here.

I would not. I'd be still running, probably.

Others come to talk, to pray, to give what news there is. They leave. I watch stars come out, one after another until the sky is full of bright threads. I do not see the dawn but waken to men running somewhere, everybody running and hollering out, and it appears that I have fallen in battle and there is a retreat, or some advance, and it don't matter in the least but forms a nice curiosity, a fine entertainment spooling by as I look on from this notch of warm earth.

But then Gus is there saying Get up, Ira, get up now. It's time.

I cannot. But I try, then do, causing the day to tip to one side.

If a battle, they'll have to win it without me.

Someone jerks me upright. Take 'im! It's his mess they're callin'. Take 'im dammit or I'll shoot you.

Harley.

Is it over? I say. The war?

No, this!

I cannot feel the ground under me and believe it must all be some dream. But since it is reasonable under the circumstances to think that, it must mean that it is not happening, none of it, and thinking it is don't make sense, but on the other hand since I am thinking it don't make sense, that might mean it does or else the rebs are pulling some show to prove how crazy we all have gotten, themselves included.

But it seems so. This snag of sticks breaking up, the river pushing on.

Ten

Lantern light. Or else I have died and come Somewhere Else.

Somebody is saying They want us crawlin' afore they'll trade for a good strong reb. Somebody else says No that ain't true. We need our boys fair and square. Somewhere in my brain I am grown wise again. These words tell me the war ain't over yet. They need their boys, still.

But could be some dream. A scare shoots through me. *Marinus*, I say.

Pull myself out of some gully of half-sleep and find him alongside me, crumpled in a heap.

Marinus, I say again.

The heap moves a little.

From the sounds of it we are on a train. And the train is moving.

I lie back and let the sensation of it wash brain if not body clean.

We are on a train, going somewhere else.

So this is some exchange, then?
Didn't say that.
Dammit! You must know something!
No sir, I do not.

The dialogue in this car. Marinus and I listen. One thing is clear. We are moving.

Why is it we have to be such knowing creatures? And when we don't or can't know, why is it we are jarred to our very roots.

Who do we think we are? Or what?

Right now I know that I know nothing. I do not know what has become of my *Soldier's Book for Leisure Moments.* I do not know what has become of my clasp knife. I pat the straw all around me. Try to remember if I dropped the book at the stream when I pushed Harley. Marinus, I say. My book. It's gone. It's a hard thing and my voice wobbles with it.

So is his book.

I pat the floor of the car, the few shreds of straw. I don't know where they are. What has become of them. Don't know how we have come to be here. Or where we're going. Or what day it might be. Or night. Or the year. Or the president's name. Or anything that counts. And don't know that it matters.

Still, my book. It wasn't anything in the scheme of things. Just some ink and paper. But how I would like to have it back.

A reb slides open the door, probably for relief from the bunch of us. We see the sun floating low in purple haze. See fields, tree-lines, gold flowers. We are all aghast at the wonder of it. Then the guard pulls the door mostly shut.

No feed in this car. Water all gone. Waste buckets filling. Men grousing.

The train slows and we go quiet, watchful. The guard slides open the door again, and we all glimpse a burnt-down station.

Sherman, one of us says.

We see rails twisted around trees.

His calling card.

Two fellows try to run. Are shot.

Then more countryside again, that purple sinking sun.

The train slows, stops. Trainmen do things. There's a clatter and we all tense, thinking the same thing — bread. Water.

And it is.

Those colors. This corn pone. Something and not nothing. And then just like that, sliding in on its own wave — hope. And body prickling awake, and brain.

It is tempting right now to believe that I am life's equal. That I measure up. That it will take me somewhere I deserve and am able to be.

The old story.

Mama! They don't have tails! They look just like our boys!

167

So says a little girl to her mama.

No we ain't got 'em anymore, ma'am, a prisoner leans out to say. Trimmed 'em off b'cause we was always steppin' on 'em in marches.

Townsfolk have come with baskets of food for the guards, but these are appropriated by our boys who stick out their hands for them. Then the baskets passed man to man and to the guards too. Biscuits, sweetmeats, bread, apples. We don't look, just grab.

Now they're bringing buckets of milk and ladles and tin cups for all of us. A dowager in black carries a pail of water from car to car, then goes back to her house nearby for more. One of our boys asks the honor of knowing her name. Mrs. J. B. Campbell, she says, and frowns at the whole lot of us. Mrs. J. B. Campbell, she repeats loudly so we can all hear.

Well Missus Campbell, a fellow says, the Army of the Potomac thanks you.

Augusta, Georgia, we learn.

When it is my turn to speak my thanks, I cannot. But I'm burgeoning with the sentiment.

Moving again. Someone claims it is 10 P.M. Might or might not be but what does it matter. We're going somewhere. Exchange,

I am thinking. It must be. Marinus holding together all right. It is peaceful until a talker starts up. There is always one such fellow. Can't bear the quiet maybe. Now this one is badgering a guard with questions. The guard is blacked-up with pitch smoke as we all are and he don't seem in a mood for chatter. The talker is telling a story about a fellow who counterfeited death, was carried to the dead-house, lay stacked up with the bodies, then was put in the trench. He'd figured they wouldn't bury him until morning, but he figured wrong. So there he is, getting buried. He goes through with it, makes a little hollow for air and waits 'em out. When he figures they are gone, he scrabbles out like a woodchuck and creeps off into the woods. So now you fellows have to post guards in the dead-house to keep even those boys from runnin'. Some of us laugh.

Who was it? I ask. Louie, I am thinking. Has to be. And that his plan. I see him now, roving through woods, coming to fields like the one we saw and throwing himself down in the sweet of it.

Don't know who it was, the fellow says. Would call him fortunate though. By God, I would.

He launches another story but a guard tells him to close his yap. When he don't, he gets

169

shoved onto others, there's a scuffle, and the talker ends up hit in the jaw and moaning.

So much for our small armistice.

Rumors and speculation. Charleston! Transports! Exchange!

Want to believe it. But they're also saying we're being evacuated on account of Sherman getting too close.

So going to another prison.

We all get gloomy pondering the sense this makes.

Hand has a gash in it. How this happened I do not know, but the sight stuns me in this flat light of somewhere.

Nail probably.

Boys have to help us maneuver, Marinus and me. Am numb. Legs, arms, hands, and so the gash not hurting, and I trick myself into believing it ain't there. Then see it is.

We're in some enclosure. They are counting and recounting. I can smell the sea as I gaze upon a vision. A fellow behind a horse and plow, turning up the earth.

It is not plain earth he's turning up. It is a race track. Marinus, I say, look. He's ploughing the race track for sweet potatoes. Gus should be here.

To think of Gus left behind somewhere draws the point of a blade across my heart.

Sunset clouds above us are all furrowed, long neat rows of them, gray and rose. Nice to watch but I am sliding down into a sink of self-pity. What would Gus do? He'd kneel and pray. Then pat the ground as if claiming it for the Union.

I do both those things and feel a little better. Can you eat your biscuit? I ask Marinus.

He shakes his head.

I take it and chew up a portion. Give it to him.

There, I say. Swallow.

He shakes his head.

Marinus, I can't bear losing another thing. You swallow that damn biscuit so I can give you another bite.

I see his scrawny throat working. All right, I say. Good. Now this.

Joke of the day: Do rebels have hearts?

No. Lost 'em when they seceded.

The reb ploughing is making our new dead line.

Shelling. Direction of the harbor. They say it's our own General Foster, shelling the town of Charleston. Don't know we're here, they say. Will he shell the race track? You damn right he will is the talk.

Too low to dig a well as many of us are doing. The water here poor, brackish. This whole area pocked with holes. No walking anywhere at night without cracking a leg bone.

You feel any better, Marinus?

Ain't played out yet.

What ain't?

The final scene.

Suppose it ain't, yet.

Nearby, boys are singing Home, Sweet Home. A shell strikes in the distance, then fire smudges the sky. Burning someone's home. Atlanta burning, half gone, maybe more. Charleston, Petersburg, Richmond, crops, barns, houses, stations, woods, the South burning like some rag soaked in kerosene.

God of the Battlefields, rescue us.

A rebel lad throws something out onto the dirt of the dead line. I step down into the loose earth and limp toward it. Pick it up. Split and sandy but still warm.

Get out of there! somebody yells. You want to get kilt?

Hear myself saying Don't care one way or another. Limp back across the furrows, hanging onto the treasure, not believing in it yet. Take a bite. Foolish tears sting, it is so sweet.

Sweet potato.

Hand stiff, festering.

The dawn a pearl and inside it, a black cut-out: sentry. Then other forms. Bell-shaped dresses. Children. And a bunch of us moving toward those shapes.

The women throw parcels toward us. The sentry turns his back. We skitter out into the dirt of the dead line, retrieve those parcels. We're quiet about it so as not to awake the others. I can make ten feet or so before playing out, then just fall over the parcel. This sentry a good one, but any minute another might come on, blow us all to the pearly gates.

Somebody drags me all the way back, a good fellow, taking time to do that. From safe ground I can watch boys dart out, back. The sentry slowly turns to us and we all go still. A parcel falls near his feet.

Please sir, one of the women is saying, give it to a prisoner.

In a polite voice he says he ain't allowed.

She lifts her child over the low track railing, then climbs it herself, a frothy swish of skirts and petticoats. They are both walking right toward the sentry.

Go back! we shout.

He aims at us.

She picks up the parcel, says something to him. He shakes his head, still looking at us.

She leans to the child. He stays with the sentry. She comes toward us.

Go back, ma'am!

She gives her parcel to the first fellow in her direct line, then turns and goes back.

He lifts out stockings, shirt, cap, biscuits. Places the biscuits on the piece of wrapping paper. We walk by him. I too have biscuits.

Boy, he says, join me for breakfast. And you, sir.

We break our bread just as shelling from the harbor starts up.

The wound not healing but black and supperating. I am getting the "raves." When I go on too long somebody pours water over my top and tries to get me to say where I belong in the compound. Which hundreth, which thousand. Marinus still in his heap. I tell myself not to wander about, but do. Must walk in my sleep. Get lost.

I'm a coward, I tell a figure all in white. So work fast now. The angel says nothing. Looks at my hand front and back. Napkin will do as a bandage, it tells me, and the bread'll make you better.

Figure I'm dreaming again and lay back, bread against my chest, though I don't know it's bread until the scent of it reaches me, and then good hand breaks the crust and I'm chewing. Then someone comes by like wind and it's gone, that bread.

He wraps the shroud around my bad hand, Marinus. You have to live, he says.

Why?

I didn't and look at me.

It's clear I'm dreaming again.

Show him your hand, he's saying. Go ahead. Show him.

But where's the hospital?

Right here.

Where?

Right here!

Point. This the hospital but that patch, no. Point. This here Union soil, that Confederate. Point. This here free earth, that, prisoner.

There ain't no hospital here.

There is, only you can't see it. I'll show him your hand, Ira.

He unwraps it. The stench about knocks us both out.

A surgeon lifts a jug of carbolic acid, letting it flow, sizzling, over the wound. Boys brace me as I sway backward, the banner of the world furling up. Waking, I see a stone jug and a packet of diarrhea powders. Drink from the jug: whiskey. Swoon backward again but along the way hearing something from Woodbury's. I shall have, I shall be, I shall become.

Take me too, I tell an orderly. Seeing as how everything is near gone, I should be too. This is foolish, I tell him. Ain't it?

He gives me more whiskey and I slide away on the heat of it.

Where's Marinus I hear myself saying, far away.

And he says Who?

And I let those words go, too.

Eleven

The fellow whistling has rose-bud cheeks. I tell him so. He laughs. Says he's told a few ladies that in his time but not a one of them ever returned the compliment.

Am I dying?

Not that I know of, he says. Your hand's just a plain mess. Might have to take it.

Take it where?

Cut it, son.

Then I'll die.

Depends. Maybe not.

It's all right.

Oh now. Not so fast.

Maybe it's all I can do. For the Union.

Might try living.

Tried.

You're in a nice sour mood.

You're not Father Blaze.

No, son. Dr. Yarmony. Rhymes with harmony. That's why I'm so good at whistlin'.

And he does.

So he's gone too?

Who might that be?

Father Blaze. Because he was a spy. Do you know where Marinus is?

No son, I don't. Let's see that hand now.

He looks, turns to some orderlies. Boys, get the jug.

They are laughing about it, the sick and not-so-sick, the surgeons, orderlies, and me too. Reb reasoning: yellow fever in the city so we have to get farther away from the 5th Georgia. And in the rain. We strike our small tents, the able help the lame, and the whole hobbling bunch of us make our removal in drizzle and low cloud and set up again on wet ground a few yards away.

We are near the stands where surgeons do their work and some officers have quarters. They shoo us away.

We move again. Fifty yards in a new direction, under some pines.

Somebody objects to something. We move again — back into the main compound. Yarmony no longer whistling, seeing how so many of us were done in for good by these removals. Oh what do I know! he raves. What do I know but that it's October 3rd and tomorrow, God willing, is a new day.

October 3rd. Something and not nothing — knowing this much. October 3rd. The 3rd of October. Leaf time, at home.

Leafy time opens. I am there. Each and every thing in its place in the shop and at home, and in the woods so much color everywhere, color to stun the heart. And everywhere some kind of design. In the leaves. The clouds. The falling of the light.

Tomorrow they aim to take my hand. A joke, maybe, in how it comes to a small thing in the end and not a big thing at all. Do not believe I am afraid of death. Only of the rutted road getting there.

Ira, you're the sorriest creature for feeling so sorry for yourself. A plain mess of sorrow when you should be glad, for here it is now, the exchange. And if certain religions are right and souls do come back in another form, maybe you'll come back as a mule and find some dignity that way.

One surgeon tells the prisoner to lie on the floor. Another puts chloroform against his nose. The third surgeon, an old fellow, kneels alongside the man and in one quick move, severs flesh and arteries, then commences sawing the bone above the elbow. Blood has fountained up onto his face, drips from his nose and chin and ears but still he saws. The other surgeon tries to sponge his face clean. In no time the arm is off, lying in a puddle of blood alongside the man. The prisoner wakes up, sees the old surgeon's chin and laughs. Look who's lost an arm, he says. Not me!

Then he's bellowing. They pour whiskey into him and then it's my turn.

The youngest of the three appraises my hand, tells me to remove my shirt. I try. It rips into pieces across the back. I stare at the wreckage. He tells me to hurry. The old bloodied one comes up, takes a glance at my hand. You crazy, boy? I don't know who he is addressing. That ain't nothin' there, he says. The third comes up, looks, then the three move away to continue the debate. No. Yes.

No. Yes.

The young one comes up. Git your shirt on.

The old surgeon is already sawing away at another fellow.

Outside, I stand in drizzle. Smell the earth. The sea. The rain. There seems a design to it.

I take long breaths.

The turmoil in my belly becomes something close to joy. But fear in there, too. Because now I have to live.

Marinus! I call. Marinus!

Other boys look up, watching me weave in and out of their camp spots, tripping over mush-tins and what-not. Clumsy, in my blanket boots.

Marinus!

I try to describe the man but we all look like one another now, brown and black as dirt, with rooty bones poking through everywhere.

Marinus! I call. I walk, then rest. Walk. Rest. Walk. Call. Rest.

I kneel alongside sleeping boys, done-up boys. Follow the perimeter of the compound, looking over the railing into the furrowed dirt of the dead line.

Growing nothing but death.

Marinus! *Marinus!*

He looks a little like General Meade, I say. Only he's gone off his head some.

They sometimes laugh at these words and it strikes me as some amusement too. How I am their entertainment now. These boys fixed on their little rafts built out of blankets, mush-tins, and a bit of talk.

Where are we all floating to?

Yarmony on his rounds. Whistles. Says to the prisoner named Hope, S-s-s-s-ing us s-something. And Hope sings, in his agreeable tenor, verses from The Sword of Bunker Hill.

He don't take it badly, either, the doctor. Those words about freemen rising up to protect the right, and God helping them so that the true flag will once again wave in the traitor's land. He walks off whistling the tune.

Marinus gone for good, I fear.

But I am looking for him, still. Won't give up until I find the pile of his bones.

The thought strikes that maybe they have already carted off those bones.

No, I say. No. No. Boys look at me but it is nothing new in here. A fellow off his head and babbling away.

Shoot those men! somebody is hollering. Somebody clearly in command. I order you to shoot, sir.

I creep closer.

A bunch along the dead line and in it too. What happens is that prospectors lose their "spots" to newcomers, then there's a regular clash and skirmish resulting in a general displacement into the dead line.

Shoot at once! a reb officer says.

A sentry is aiming his weapon at a pile of boys. There's no room for them to maneuver out of there.

Fire your weapon, sir!

I try to get back but others have come up behind me. We are all packed in tight and surging closer to the dead line ourselves.

Fire!

A lady at the far railing greets the colonel.

Mornin', Colonel Robson!

The sentry has his musket aimed but his head is down as if he's waiting to be shot himself. Other ladies arrive. I can't see to be certain, but know they must be carrying parcels.

The nabob pushes off without returning cordialities.

The sentry looks up at the bunch of us. Says Don't a one of you boys try crossin' this line. You do, yer all dead men.

We cheer him.

The next day he ain't there. Fear he's a dead man himself.

They have built large fires around the perimeter of the track. The air smokes with pitch pine. We're all black as savages, rebs and prisoners alike.

Yarmony tells me the hand is better. I will live — for a while yet. In the meantime can I help him?

I hesitate a little.

We're opening a fever ward, he says. Here's your chance. He don't look at me full on. I know what it means.

Means if I want to go, here is my chance.

He's begging. Nobody else wants that work.

I am just low enough about not finding Marinus to say all right.

Now I scout the compound for the sick and the dying. Remember to call his name. The sound of that name hangs there in the day for a while, then is gone.

Dr. Yarmony studied medicine in New York and would like to go back there after the war. Nights, before sleep, I pretend I am Dr. Yarmony in New York, a young lady on my arm. I swing a walking stick in the park. I help her in and out of carriages. I know when to applaud at entertainments and how to speak in drawing rooms. Know how to cut open a man to save him. All these things figure in dreams and more, shaming things, frightening things. I awake sweaty and aching with hunger and cold, usually lying burrowed in alongside somebody.

Awake feeling that hope is foolish. Foolish to believe in some change for the better. Foolish to think I'll find Marinus. Foolish to think this war will end. Foolish, any kind of faith at all. Where is Sherman? Nobody knows for sure. Where are Grant and Lee? Where are the fellows who can stop all this?

Not in here.

What I can do: Mark a fellow with a piece of chalk. Orderlies follow me with a stretcher. Haul off the feverish ones.

What I can do: Check my gums daily for blood. Check my urine for albumin.

What I can do: Live to be a footprint. Maybe.

Meaning is a ladder we make, ain't it? Takes us high into the sky where it stops.

Just like that.

Here we are, then.

But the climb nice, if not the view below.

Now I sound like Marinus.

I am at the track scouting for him again. I see a blond boy standing part way in the dead line. Come on, he calls. Got fruits and bread and a piece of dried beef. Get a bit closer so you can catch 'em. I am trying to figure out why there ain't any others around and why the ploughed earth hasn't a single footstep in it. It's all right, the boy says, he ain't around here, that sentry. You're safe. If you eat something, you'll get stronger. You'll make it.

He is right. It is finally just a question of food. Maybe food is the secret of hope.

I step onto the track. Something leaves me, some tied-up tightness. I want to give over to the loosening, the slackening.

I hear Marinus say *Ira*.

But it ain't him, I know. He's dead. Leave me alone, Marinus, I say. Dead or alive, you are just a trouble to a fellow.

The boy is telling me that with food I may amount up yet. I cannot disagree.

In his hands a slice of bread with creamery butter. Apples. Salt pork and beef.

I fall before I can reach these things. A battle ensues. Shot. Hollering.

Hear Marinus telling me there is no boy there, never was, but I cannot believe a dead man.

Wake up in the fever ward. Marinus alongside me. They say he was lying somewheres a way off. Have a new wound that needs cauterizing. Along chin and neck. Here we are again, and I am glad to see the fellow yet it is still bad as any dream.

And as strange, I hold a pen in hand. Brown and gold, tortoise-shell.

Marinus tells me Yarmony has given it to me since I have been driving him over the edge complaining about how many things I have lost.

Now a sutler is passing through the ward. Eyes the pen.

You got anythin' to trade, boy?

No, I say.

Nice pen there. Give you two of my best

for it. He holds up an apple the color of Yarmony's cheeks.

Can't, I say.

He digs in his box. Holds up another, bigger than the first.

No sir, I say.

No? You think you got a hair-loom there, but hair-looms don't do a bit of good in here, you know that?

Know it.

I know the exact tree these here come off of. Can't find a better apple in the Confederacy. You find a single worm, I'll trade two apples for it tomorrow.

I am turned mute. In my hand, tight, is the pen. It is possible to be a footprint with a pen. This I tell the sutler.

Yer gone crazy, boy.

Yes sir, I say.

He starts walking. Stops. Comes back. Here, he says, and tosses me a slice. So you'll know what yer missin'.

I hold the juice and sweetness in my mouth long as I can while down the ward he goes, calling to dead men Apples! The best apples!

Yarmony tells us he can't get medicines. Shell hit the medical purveyor's office.

Half the morning he has been trying to

get a boy to swallow a pulped-up radish. The boy's name is Davey. Has scurvy so bad he is near frozen solid. Yarmony no longer whistling. Is short with all of us. When he asks Hope to sing something, he don't stutter.

Hope sings Christmas tunes. Davey wants 'em.

We don't.

Today forty stronger boys sent back out in exchange for forty sick ones. In most cases we can't tell the difference.

Merry Christmas, boys.

It is not the right time to do this but I haul myself up and go over to Yarmony. Maybe I think the thought will slide away for good if I don't.

Please sir, I say. Then stop. Can't bring myself to beg. And he needs to be off fixing boys. But I say it fast. Paper. Envelope. Stamp.

He takes it in. Seems I have asked for gold bullion.

Today he dropped those items alongside me. Come, Hope. S-s-s-ing.

Hedgehogs, Yarmony says.

Does he mean the prisoners? It ain't like him to fool in that way. When guards try to rally us, saying General Foster knows we're

188

here but don't care, Yarmony says he don't know. So it makes no sense now for him to be calling us hedgehogs.

Already three thousand of us gone. This place turning into a ruined race track again.

Florence, we hear. Another prison there. Since this is the majority rumor, Marinus and I don't believe it. We say they are going off for an exchange somewhere. We try not believing that, either. If there is a way of tricking whatever powers there are, we are trying to find it.

Hedgehogs, Yarmony says again. Do I know that saying about hedgehogs and foxes?

No sir, I do not.

S-s-s-something about tricks, he says, and goes off to get some of our boys ready for the removal.

He is not coming with us. He is going to stay in the city.

This makes me a little done up but then what don't?

Yet how is it that he can be talking about hedgehogs and foxes, with yellow fever raging and everything falling apart inside here and without too, probably?

Oh we are brainless ejeets. Louie would have caught on at once. Hedgehogs!

Hard not to laugh about it, though, in these creaking cars taking us somewhere else.

Boys hiding themselves in holes during the removal, some only a few feet wide, others no wider than a boot. Holes not too wet, maybe. Boys being pulled out, rabbits from a hat, by rebs going from one to another, poking around with sticks. Seeing them wandering over the empty grounds, we wondered what they were looking for. Then came a shout as guards ran to a hole and pulled out some hapless hedgehog.

But surely they do not find each and every one. Surely some of them hedgehogs are sliding through the streets of Charleston right now, heading for our ships.

I close my eyes and am waiting in the dark. Numb and sore from being all doubled up. Then I'm crawling up out of that hole and have to wait for blood to push through the collapsed parts of me. I uncrumple like a piece of paper.

No use even thinking it. Marinus, I say, have some of this clean water. I raise his head to see if he's still among the living.

He is.

Vermin, as usual, carry too many guns for our lines. I scratch myself silly. I am a coat of burrs. I try not to draw blood, scratching.

Who do you want, sir? somebody is saying in this car. Mr. Lincoln or General McClellan? The war will end, you know, if the General wins. He'll cut them loose for sure. Why not? What's the good of 'em?

For a moment I think they are talking about Marinus cutting the Confederate states loose. In my thoughts, I picture Marinus as a surgeon, sawing away.

Who you voting for, boy? a fellow asks.

Abe, I say. If I had a hundred votes, I say, I would cast them all for Abe.

Twelve

Doors rumble open. Sharp cold air. We stir, but not all of us, and I know that many have gone ahead on their own journeys.

Marinus, I say.

And he says We owe a cock to — Somebody. Can't make out the fancy word. Do not neglect to pay it, he says.

Or some nonsense like that.

Outside, the quiet hums. The dark thick. Guards order us out.

A scare burns through me. Too much trouble for them, sick. Not enough food. No place, no room for us here. The North not wanting us either. Not wanting to send mended rebs back to the fight.

Shooting us makes sense.

Which may be why, probably, they won't.

Have Marinus in a stretcher. We slide it down an embankment. Feet struggle through corn stubble.

Hard going.

Beans'n bacon, I think. Corn pone. Rice cakes. Beef. Tent.

Imagining all this just ahead, I trip and stumble. And seeing, too, Grant and Sherman in their own tents on this hard night, figuring how to invade Charleston, which wasn't threatened by yellow fever at all but by our boys moving in from the sea and from the land. A pincer to squeeze the life out of the Confederacy.

So: losing us, the rebs would lose thousands of their own. Therefore &ct. this removal.

When a man has nothing else but his brain, he can at least think.

For the silly show of it.

Field stretches on. We do our best in it. Marinus moans from time to time and I am assured.

We come to no tents, no campsite, no prison, no beans and bacon, no blankets or water. We halt though there is no apparent reason for doing so. Guards busy themselves hemming us around with fires. We get Marinus close to one, then lay flanking him.

Caesar in Gaul, he says.

The other orderly, Abraham Sommers, tears up a cornstalk in his way. When I close my eyes, I see rebs heaving all our remains into them fires sweeping up into the cold. Digging'll be too hard, in this hard earth.

Marinus murmuring in some foreign tongue. Then it's quiet, except for the crackle of fires and Abraham Sommers' whistling breath.

Just before dawn the moon hangs low over the field. That moon the same color as the fires. Under it, stockade walls.

Seems to be Camp Sumter, at Andersonville. Soon we're marching toward it.

Come to a wall of unhewn tree trunks dripping resin. At each corner of the pen is a squared-off platform for heavy guns. Aimed inward. At the enemy there.

The gate swings open easily enough.

Boys rush forward to ask who we are, where we're from and what's the news. Others are uprooting stumps on hillsides inside here. I cannot remember there being any trees in Camp Sumter but I see how much firewood they will make. Stacks of pine branches tell me *roof.*

I point out these advantages to Marinus. In the time of Cicero, he tells us, the Romans would not say the words They are dead but rather, They did live.

The first way, he says, too strong. Unlucky.

I tell him not to start growling and muddying my brain and making things worse.

He gives his wink.

Abraham Sommers is taken with Marinus's ability to jaw when he wants to. He wishes he could. Then he'd jaw his way out of here.

The boys tell us it is not Camp Sumter, but Florence, in South Carolina.

Anything with South in it, Abraham Sommers says, I don't want.

Inside here we are a divided country. Those who have forsworn their allegiance to the United States government by swearing allegiance to the Confederacy, and those of us who so far have not.

The newly-sworn ones seem worse off, body and spirit, than us. They are like spavined horses. Bony, shaking, and some with the unhinged eye of madmen. They are supposed to get new clothing and boots, medicine and food. These promises are all that keep them moored to the living, it seems. They bunch together like cattle in a storm. They watch us, those who have any wit left, with suspicion. Sometimes a fellow who has not yet made up his mind which way to go will heave himself down on the ground and begin weeping. We sometimes hoot these boys, though I do not care much for myself when I do it. Hoot them, saying their wives and families ain't gonna have them back. Some of us in favor of forgiving them. Live and let live. Saying it is just a trick to escape and not a bad one at that.

Those who forgive probably are tempted

to do the same thing. I am. When I think of the word escape, I feel temptation in my throat, in the thirst there, the burn, and behind my eyes. The pictures there. Join! I tell myself. Join the CSA.

But there is Marinus. Not much fit to join anything except the dead.

And I don't know as I could stomach having a CSA uniform next to my skin. Maybe before, but not now.

Am learning that hatred is a kind of bread, hard and stale, but bread all the same. Keeps the blood flowing nearly as good as hope.

What is surprising is the degree to which I can hate. I am near becoming hate-ful. That is, full of it, body and brain. Is it not a wonder how we can do that and so little of anything else?

Marinus chirping again, more or less. Tells me I am an idolator of the old. What in deuce is that? I say. He says Wouldn't let me go. Who's talking! I say. You're my friend, like it or not. That's what I mean, he says, idolatry. Abraham Sommers gives a long sigh. He's mopping his tin plate with a darkened finger. He licks the finger, then licks the plate. Marinus looks up into the branches I have woven for our roof. We are directly under platform supports for one of the big guns.

We are fortunate, boys, to have this, Abraham Sommers says. Prisoners over in Richmond, I been hearing, draw rations in their boots if they don't have mush-tins. Seems a bonus, don't it? He rubs the plate. Twirls finger around its rim.

Marinus puts in One can say that the tragedy of humankind is Less and More.

Abraham Sommers wants to know if he was some kind of preacher once.

Don't know, I say. He won't tell.

Reminds me of a sick dog we once had. All's it could do was walk in circles.

I don't like talking about Marinus this way, with him right there and all. I ask Abraham Sommers if he thinks they'll throw our boys in against Sherman.

Want to join? he says.

Hard for me to say a word then.

Chaff in a fan blade, he says. Is what they'll be. Chaff in a blade unless they run pretty quick.

Call me Less, Marinus says. And you can be More.

It's a pity, Abraham Sommers says, but I seen 'em worse.

What's our number again? I ask him. I'm always forgetting it.

Nine and seven, he says. The lucky ones. Nine thousand. Seven hundred.

Tossed into the bin once more like so many poor apples, but they're counting and sorting, sorting and counting all the same. We have just gone through another rigamarole to see if we are bad enough to get in the hospital here.

Abraham says now If they don't take me in there, I know one thing. I am going to join, Ira. Won't last the winter otherwise with this chest of mine. Get some good feeds, then run. Don't know but that I'll be home in a couple two three weeks.

You'll wear their uniform?

What's to bother? Cloth is cloth. Anything's better'n these rags. You kin come with me. I'll see you get back home and that's a promise. Plenty of strength left in this old apple tree.

The words remind me that I am half-naked in my torn shirt and that winter is nearby, waiting to ambush. Abraham's gray hair reminds me of Gus. His voice seems almost Louie's.

You don't need no anchor now, boy. Time's getting too damn short. No sense turnin' over the same bit of ground day after day.

That seems right, I say.

Sure! And I'm on the square. We can do it.

He starts coughing bad and I wonder. He must have been a big man once. His head and hands still are. I tell him maybe he could find another fellow to join with.

He says a man needs somebody he can trust.

My hand's no good, I say.

That hand'll hold. They won't care about that hand. Besides, they might fix it for you.

Marinus tells me I should go.

Abraham promises we'll make it.

Marinus says it is the reasonable course.

Sure, Abraham says. Any man can see it.

All this shot coming too heavy for me. I'll think on it, I say.

Well, Abraham says, I ain't a drinkin' man nor a thinkin' one. A little bit a each is all a man needs. Too much and you go under.

Marinus calls him wisdom personified.

I tell him to keep quiet. I tell him he ain't any help.

And he ain't.

We wait at the main gate, we Charleston boys, while the sick from Florence take our measure. Worse off than me or not?

Gangrene smells like any sort of rotting flesh, man or critter. It is a sweet-dark smell to make you gag.

199

Ain't this a stench, boy? Abraham says.

It is — in every way. One fellow with gangrene is eyeing me, wondering, I suppose, why I'm even there. So I let my hand hang in the open for the man to see though I would rather have it covered and hidden from all this.

It should help make up your mind, Abraham says.

I don't answer him because I still can't. You read about people like saints and wonder about them. It seems to me now that being a saint is like being a hero. In each case there's some denying involved, a big denying. Well, I ain't a saint or any hero. I want good things bad as any man. Food and warmth and no more pain. A saint or a hero might give up his place here at the gate so somebody else can get into the hospital. A hero might be glad of the chance to die of gangrene so a rebel will never make it back to his regiment. Would a hero sign the CSA oath of allegiance? Would Gus?

No.

Would Grant? Would Sherman?

No two times.

Or would they — and then try to escape back to their lines?

It is too much for me, the now of this, my thoughts skittering away from me and I staggering after them. Far away, someone is hanging onto my hand, holding it to the light.

I hear myself trying to be a hero, trying to say I don't need to go, but my teeth are bumping and seem about to slide out one after another.

Somebody pushes me to one side. Abraham to another. Rebs start loading stretchers into wagons, and healthy-looking Northern boys, it appears, fan out among us separating the sheep from the goats.

Abraham is calling my name, saying I'm making a mistake. He hollers that I am a fool.

That is one thing I do know. But to hear it publicly declaimed makes my face hot, my heart a burdensome weight. I look over there and get a glimpse of his big head, the white hair. It is the last I see of him.

Marinus says he is right and I am wrong. I should go.

But we're going somewhere else and it takes up attention nicely. Wagons bumping and splashing through ruts. Wind carrying the sounds of the hurt. I am walking and smelling leaf-decay and cold mud now instead of gangrene. And then something else.

It comes to me, the what-else. Charred logs, sticks, lumber, burnt-over woods. The smell of a big burning somewhere.

The sun is a Confederate sun, angling down from a line of gray cloud on high.

Do not take it as a good omen.

Thirteen

A surgeon studies my hand. He is taking so long I am stiffening up, by this warm kerosene lamp. Want to cry like a fool. Why? Because he is too close and is taking so much care. He is rendering me into a weepy girl.

A reb, I tell myself. Think of Gus. Think of Willy. This fellow don't care a bean for *you*.

None of it does much good. The way he's acting you'd think we were blood brothers.

Ira, he says, and the sound of my name spoken by this rebel wreaks havoc on me. What did they do for this at Charleston? he asks.

Now I shame myself with tears.

After a while I can talk. Cauterizing. Carbolic acid. They almost cut.

He pretends not to notice the weepiness. Glad they didn't, he says. He draws in a breath, lets it out. Looks again at the black knuckles, the swollen-tight-and-about-to-burst skin.

Looked worse before, I say. You could see the gangrene.

I'm afraid we'll have to cauterize again, he says. But with some clean compresses and decent food, you might be out of the woods soon.

I chance a straight look at him to see if this is a joke. It don't seem to be. He is a thin man. Homely, you would say. Don't have much hair, his skin is sallow and bunchy and oily, all wrinkled around the eyes and blue-black there. His skull under that frail hair looks knobby. Yet so much life seems to be pouring from his hand directly into mine.

I tell myself to fight it. They only betray you, the rebels. Yarmony could have told me straight out and not fooled with that hedgehog story.

He releases my hand. Don't give up now, he says.

I leave the shed blind to everything.

These sheds. Had us all in a frenzy of speculation earlier when we saw them from the rutted road. They have pine-branch roofs and board walls on three sides. Was something to behold.

Still is.

I go into our ward and lie face-down on pine branches, smell their pitchy smell.

Marinus says What's the matter?

Hate him, I say.

Who?

That surgeon.

What did he do?

Looked at my hand.

Marinus sighs. He tells me I'm a mess, but I should hate the fellow if I want. It's good entertainment.

I ask if he cares about anything. He says No he don't.

So why are you here? I ask him.

He tells me not to try to figure everything out.

We have a regular sally going and it's good. Marinus, I say. It's better when we talk, ain't it?

Not much, he says.

And that's the end of it.

I awake to some clanking and clatter. It appears to be an orderly with a bucket of steaming soup.

We sit up. We don't believe a fraction of it. Not even when we raise mush-tins and smell the tomatoes.

Clear we have gotten into the wrong batch.

I try a joke. Do you think they'll give us some bounty for joining up?

He says So how do you feel about him now?

Who?

That surgeon.

I don't say a word then.

Don't get besotted, he tells me. As with

that priest of yours.

Do you remember his name, Marinus? I have forgotten.

Arma virumque cano, he says.

No, I say. That wasn't it.

It means I sing of arms and the man.

Don't seem much to sing about.

Tell that to Publius Vergilius Maro.

Who's he?

Was. A poet.

You're feeling sparky, ain't you. So he liked war, did he?

Liked to imagine the heroic scale of things, anyway. But he died of fever when he was fifty-one. I'm fifty-one.

But you're not going to die of it.

Marinus is quiet.

Open your mouth, I say.

He raises his upper lip slightly.

It's not bad, I say, lying.

Look again, he says.

I can't see any blood.

I'm going yellow.

Only a little bit. It might be mild.

Might. But then again —

Let's think of right now, I say. Let's do like Gus would do. Think of right now and don't go no further.

A foggy drizzle beads the overhanging branches, drips down. But we are dry. We have a roof. Pine branches to sleep on. A blanket. It may be October or it may be November, but we are dry and with full bellies. Warm. Things are sliding away. The priest's name. Gus's last name. And Louie gone, too. Maybe Charleston. Maybe pulled from a well-hole. Maybe run from the burial grounds. What kind of footprint will I be if I can't remember a damn thing.

Unless a crazy madman footprint. Needles prick me from behind the eyes, then in legs, arms. Hand.

I smell the branches. Touch the blanket. Listen for what I can hear, the music in it, the plinking of drops, the rustle of branches under me, their turpentine smell. Then I am with Dr. Strother again and he is holding onto my hand, willing life into the dead heart of it.

I make a fist, open it. The fingers rise more or less in the right way. I make a fist again. Several days of cauterizing, clean compresses, and good food have worked this miracle.

So, Dr. Strother says. The word is a tired exhalation.

My throat too tight, I say what I have been practicing all week to say — that I want to help him.

How? he asks. He is testing each joint slowly and with great care.

An orderly, I creak out. I am seeing the oak bins, again, the prescription case, the red show globes. I have worked, I say from this dream, for an apothecary.

Impossible, it seems, that I have spoken such a mouthful of a word, something so ponderous and belonging to the other world.

He asks if I can define mercurous chloride.

I cannot, it seems. Those words off sitting in some distance and beckoning. You know me! But I don't. Know only that I should.

It is a — I take a guess . . . purgative. Then know I am right. Not for diarrhea, I say.

Oh? he says. What would you prescribe?

I am taken aback by his bantering tone. Does he prescribe that too? Words spin through me, remnants of my lost life. I pick one. *Paregoric.* Then others. *Camphorated tincture of opium. Quinine . . . sulfate.*

You're right, he says, not looking up from the hand. Finally he surrenders it and gives our talk full attention.

Am I principled? he wants to know.

He repeats the question, substituting the word honest.

I don't know what to say to that. I cannot tell him a part without the whole. I tell him everything. The pharmacy. Gabrielle. William Bonhoffer. J. L. Casey. The Pinkerton detectives. The reports. The running away. So no, I say. I am neither principled nor honest. I am a thief and a liar. In truth not much of a fellow at all. I don't amount up but all the same might be of some use. I tell him about Abraham Sommers and how I wanted to sign too, for food.

He don't seem to hear this part. You acted, he says, out of love. Not for personal gain. You were being loyal to that.

I know what Marinus would say to this. He would say Lo, the mind at work twisting and burrowing a way out! — or some such. But that is what the doctor's words seem to me to be doing. Twisting and tweedling a way out.

I say It was wrong, what I did.

Do you know, he says, that we have some of those drugs here, now? — I am quite sure of it.

I go quiet, reddening, face, neck, ears. Loyalty, he goes on. One hardly knows these days. He rubs the loose folds under his eyes with fingers of both hands. I know he needs to be back in the wards, working. He does not stint on the work, stays long after the other surgeons all leave for their quarters. He often sleeps in one of the sheds.

Words come. I give them to this man. You have my loyalty, I say.

His voice is parched. Scratches out. He says he believes me. We shake hands on it. He's about to leave but goes to a cupboard and pulls out boots, jacket, and gray shirt. See if these fit. If not let me know. Then he is gone.

I look at my new uniform. Touch the good cloth, warm to my hand. Begin undressing.

Head-Quarters, Military Prison. Florence, South Carolina. October 30, 1864. I, Ira Cahill Stevens (enlisted as Jim Kiefer), Private, a paroled prisoner of war, do hereby pledge my word of honor that I will not violate my parole by going beyond one-half mile from the hospital limits.

I sign this document in the presence of a rebel lieutenant colonel and several other officers. I am wearing my new uniform and boots, too big for me. My right hand feels stiff and unpracticed as I form the letters of my name, sinking into the remembered shape of it. Ira Cahill Stevens, a paroled prisoner of war, but no rebel getting back to his regiment because of it. I walk out into sunshine, fitting myself into this new person. A paroled prisoner not going home but somehow, it seems, already there.

It holds, the happiness.

We hardly know what the reb sergeant is going on about. He jokes one minute, bullies the next. He looks and acts like a tipsy fellow. Woods, he's saying now, and cross-cut marks on trees, and if we run like rabbits we'll surely pay for it. He is skinny as us. Has a frayed, sand-colored moustache that curls down over his mouth. Everything about him quivers or twitches. Eyelids. Chin. Face. Moustache. Hands. Even his skinny legs. He is taking us on a tour of the hospital grounds, telling us to pay close attention. He flings himself around to face us every so often. Struts and gives way to some kind of bellowing oratory.

God save us from these weasely sergeants. I do not trust small men in power. Lieutenant Davis was not small, nor was Yarmony. Dr. Strother is thin but not weasely. This sergeant must believe he is one of God's chosen in the Promised Land. Now he is fairly dancing, telling us of some surprise he has rigged. One we damn well better like.

At the guard's log house, the door opens and a prisoner is shoved out by two guards. The Weasel denounces him in his thin-voiced oratory, while the one guard tosses a rope over the roof beam jutting out above the door. The Weasel is saying how the fellow had gotten himself nice and situated, fixed up on their feed and med-cin, then upped and ran one day. So now he pays.

Guards have the fellow stand on a crate, tie the ends of the rope somehow to his thumbs, then pull away the crate. The fellow's arms jerk up and backward. His body doubles over forward. His long hair sways in the breeze.

Take a nice long look, boys! the Weasel says. See it don't pay, runnin'.

We can see how the hanging man is trying not to utter any sound, but finally it gets the best of him. Christ have mercy! he hollers out.

A fellow next to me, Calvin Forrest, whose hair has all but completely fallen out, turns around and stands staring at the distant woods. Then so do all eleven of us. I am hoping the poor boy up there ain't thinking we're turning away from him — only from the spectacle the rebs are making of his misery.

The woods look red to me.

Don't like it, boys? the Weasel whinnies out. Don't blame you. But I want you all to turn back around and take a good long look, so you don't forget.

We don't turn.

You boys want to get kicked back in that pen?

We still don't turn.

Get some more rope, the Weasel hollers.

We turn. One by one we turn back.

The Weasel gives a dreary laugh.

The hanging man's arms look broken. Spittle coming down off the long hair.

We are marching away. Boys! the fellow moans. Help me.

We keep going.

I cannot see anything but that hanging man. I don't know where I am. Nor do I care. Our ward-master, another prisoner, is telling us something, but I do not care what it is. I am sick to my core with all this. Sick and done up and raging away like a wind-storm inside.

Calvin Forrest nudges me to look. I do not want to but do finally. Somebody else is talking now. And we are in a log house fitted up as a dispensary. I smell herbs. Wood burning in a stove. The pine boards under our feet are a clean yellow. The log walls are chinked. The window clean. Board shelves hold a wealth of shirts, blankets, hats, shoes, slippers, stockings, quilts, dressing gowns. Tins of condensed coffee and milk, tomatoes, extract of beef, and other foods. There are barrels of tree bark, oak, sweet gum, persimmons, wild cherry, all clearly labeled. Behind the man who is now talking, there are shelves holding, I guess, all the drugs. The fellow don't look starved. He is of normal size, full-bellied and filled out, but a Northern boy like us. And he is talking to us as if we were his equal and all this was perfectly natural.

Outside, I ask Calvin Forrest what we are supposed to do. He chastises me for not listening. Hurriedly tells me how we take orders from our ward-master, then draw the requested supplies from the dispensary and give them to the ward-master, who keeps accounts.

That is not hard for my brain to keep ahold of. But what about the woods? I say.

Ira, didn't you hear nothin'? We can go in the woods when Burrell Thomas says he needs such and such. We can't go beyond the crosses on the trees. That's the dead line. If we do, we'll be dragged back by guards quiet as snakes. Dragged back and strung up. Try it a second time and we are dead men.

The woods. It is near all I can think about. Going into those woods. Smelling them. Seeing them. And how long it'll be before Burrell Thomas asks me to go.

Is it because I want to escape now? Try it?

I don't know. Just know I want them woods.

Then I see that hanging fellow and think how I have sold my soul for sure this time.

Shock leaves me unable to move a step. There is Dr. Strother on a cot, blanket over him. Resting, I tell myself. Fatigued himself the night before and so just resting.

I call his name, then regret waking him. The whites of his eyes are stained yellow, the rims blood-red.

Ira, he says.

I tell him I am sorry for waking him.

I was awake, he says. I was thinking.

Did you stay up all night again?

No.

But you're tired all the same.

Best keep some distance between us.

He raises his lip and I see teeth awash in blood.

Scurvy, I say, stiffening again with shock.

A poor diagnosis, he says and smiles a little.

There's quinine here, sir. You will have it beat. You just need rest. You've been going too hard each and every day. You —

Ira, he says.

Yes, sir?

It'll be bad. You ready?

I catch my breath. Say I am.

You're not afraid?

No, sir.

But I am — for him.

Dr. Cyrus Jewell replaces me. Will you give him your — He closes his eyes, rests a while . . . loyalty as you have given it to me?

Yes, sir, I tell him. Right now I would tell him whatever he needs to hear. But it is not a lie, neither. I will do anything for this man.

Thank you, he says. Lets his eyes shut again.

I am rushing in one direction, then another, looking for Bill, the ward-master. I need to holler, curse the devil, need to run immediately to the dispensary.

Find Bill at last, then run to the dispensary, passing the guard house. The Weasel hollers Look out there, boy. Y'don't wanta do too much runnin' now.

The list in my hand says blankets, three. Quinine, fifteen grains. Beef extract, two tins. Tomatoes, two tins.

It is good, seeing Burrell Thomas rushing about, filling this order. Good running back, arms loaded up with it all.

Dr. Jewell shouts Fine namesake, Calvin!

He is an overflowing, overblown man whose heavy gold watch chain seems stretched to the limit at his ballooning waist. You one of the reprobate? Dr. Jewell goes on, or one of the elect. He pronounces it ree-pro-bate.

Calvin Forrest is standing awkwardly with a full bucket of waste. Neither, sir. I'm a ward steward.

Dr. Jewell snorts out a laugh. The fellow can tell a joke! he says. What's happened to all yer hair?

Calvin says he don't know.

Shorn like a lamb. Clean as a lady's beehind.

A patient laughs, which is what Dr. Jewell is waiting for. His own laugh now sounds like a drum beaten.

How about politically speaking? One of the ree-probate or one of them elect?

Don't know, sir.

You believe you all will win the war, r'not?

I believe we will, sir.

You do.

Yes, sir.

Why so?

Because we're on the side of right.

I give Calvin huge credit for this. He is not selling his soul.

And right makes might? Dr. Jewell says. He glances at the patient who laughed before.

Well sir — Slavery. It's wrong.

You believe, then, it's yer destiny to win?

Yes sir. Maybe.

Maybe! Oh, wonderful! So you must see yerself as one of the elect politically speaking and possibly the other which way around too. Know something?

Calvin Forrest keeps quiet.

Yer wrong. Dead wrong. Is this how the Good Lord treats His elect?

I don't know, sir.

I don't think so. No sir. For my life I don't believe He'd allow all this.

The doctor's arms billow outward.

Tell you a secret, Calvin. I believe we're right. We of the South are the elect. Now how about that?

You have a right, sir, to believe that.

Ah-ha! Hear that, boys? The fellow agrees. States' Rights! Tell that to yer puffed-up president, why don't you.

Dr. Jewell gives the patient at his feet a cursory look before moving on through the ward, arms angled out from the bulk of him sailing away.

I have named him the Bullfrog, and I entertain Marinus with stories about him. How he don't even look much at the patients. How he tipples, out behind the wards.

Marinus says His foot shall slide in due time.

A remark that becomes famous in our ward. We all take it to mean not only Dr. Cyrus Jewell but the Confederacy as well, for another of his names, given to him by both patients and stewards, is Mr. Secession. He likes to boast how he is from Kentucky and was one of the first advocates of the Secessionist Act. I believe the man knows nothing about medicine and so yawps on as he does in order to get through the day without ever having to treat a one of us. Or maybe he considers it disloyal treating us. I am wondering how the fellow came to be assigned to a prison camp. Too poor a physician to treat any of the elect?

I hope Dr. Strother does not sense it in me. My hatred of the Bullfrog. I have to give Dr. Strother daily reports and try to be neutral about it all. Tonight, though, Dr. Strother is not asking for any reports so I tell him a story that has come back to me from my long-gone book. It is about how once the Romans worked hard to fortify their settlements along the Rhine against the Rhinelanders, and then later these fortified camps became German towns. Why I should remember that I do not know. But it makes up a nice mess of words to say, anyhow.

Strange, too, that it should come back to me like that when so much else seems lost for good.

It is something of a diversion for I want to run from the sight of him. He is all wet and looks worse than ever. When he tries to turn on his other side, the effort makes him heave black vomit over the blanket. It is mostly black blood.

I go for a clean blanket, roll up the other and throw it into a fire. I bring water and a cloth.

He tries to tell me something. I tell him not to tire himself with talk. Then he says We don't know how to die, or live, either. He tells me to go.

This time, I say, I am disobeying him.

Some of the black stuff gets onto my hands but I do not care. I am too angry for fear. I am saying to myself Let this man live. Let this one man live. Take me but let him live. Take the Bullfrog but let him live. Take the Weasel. Take us all, dammit, but let him live.

I have no heirs, he says. I had my work —

I beg him to stop talking. I tell him it will be all right, with the quinine.

No, he says. He asks me to remember him.

You're not —

Will you?

Yes, sir, I say and put my hand on his shoulder, willing the cyclone in me to swirl into him and throw the fever into retreat.

You'll live, he tells me, and carry on. Won't you? You'll live and remember me. Remember it all. You'll do that, Ira, for me —

Yes, sir, I say, hanging onto him.

Burrell Thomas picks today to send me out into the woods. Every sweet its sour. Every sour its sweet. He wants 'simmons berries. Tells me how to find them. Then I am in the woods, in shivery undergrowth and big trees. In wind and with quiet living things that have nothing to do with us. I walk on wet pine needles and mossy stone. I kneel down and claim it all for the Union. Hold rummagy leaves to my face. Be a weepy girl for a while.

I am aware of the quiet, the aloneness. There is peace here, a peace having nothing to do with us. Not needing us. Not even wanting us, as we want it and want these woods.

I do not blame it for not wanting us. For first thing you know, we will ruin it.

I want to stay here forever.

But then I see a big cross-cut mark on a tree. The X is scored deep into the pine, sap congealing white around it. Reminds me of

221

a blind man's eye, crusted-over and sealed shut. Reminds me of myself. Of us. The whole sour mess of us.

I walk laterally to get a sense of direction. I am not looking for 'simmons berries as I should be doing. I am being tempted and know it. Come to another big scored tree. Sit down against it.

Try to think, even though I know better than to do such a foolish thing.

Hear a shuffling and scratching. Hear a reel or jig played on a harmonica.

I keep still. A guard passes about ten feet away from me. Stops suddenly, swirls around. Looks squarely at me.

Want to run, boy? he says. Give you a fair chance.

He looks fit and able to chase anyone to Kingdom Come.

In this fog it'll be easy, he says.

The fog seems higher up in the trees, though. I don't say anything.

Sure, he says. I'll just finish my tune. Give you a good start.

Not sure of the way.

That way, he says. Go downhill and then come to a plank road and you'll want to turn to your left.

Where's it go?

North.

What about you?

Nothin'll happen to me. Bunch of us here. Lots to share the blame.

You want me to escape?

Didn't say that, now.

His hat is pulled low. I can't tell how old he is. Whether sore-used or not.

He starts playing the tune again. Strange and slow.

I am seeing Dr. Strother on his cot. Marinus on his pallet.

I go back. I am chilled to my bones, knowing that the fellow only wanted to hunt me down. Play some game. And chilled to my bones knowing that is not why I am going back. Loyalty, it seems, is a prison strong as any.

Took you god-awful long, Ira, Burrell Thomas says. Get lost?

Had some trouble findin' them.

Your ward-master was in here lookin' for you. The doctor died.

I go back and stand where his cot was. That's burned too by now, and the blankets and all.

Too bad, ain't it? Dr. Jewell says, coming up. Well the good go first in this man's world. Least he be out of it now.

The empty spot is expanding, overflooding

shed, hospital, prison camp, woods, making it all some empty place, and I am just standing here in it. Just standing here thinking how nothing needs to be and yet is, my Lord, it is something. It is something and not nothing.

But why is it you see that clear only when it is gone for good?

Fourteen

Battle of the Bed Sheets we are calling it.

Two hundred bed sheets from the U.S. Sanitary Commision have arrived. Excellent white cotton. Burrell Thomas is a boy on Christmas morning until we point out that we have no beds in the hospital. What are we supposed to do with them? — put 'em on the ground? or on pine branches to get sticky?

Bandages, one of us says. Burrell Thomas's face wrinkles in his speculative frown. I'll be damned, he says, if I'll distribute a one of them until I can thresh things out here.

Burrell! a ward-master hollers, you ain't gonna part with them sheets even if you had two hundred mahogany bedsteads to put 'em on!

Make yerself a nice white, suit, Burrell, and git yourself married.

How about some tablecloths!

A wedding dress, Burrell. Fellow never knows!

Sails, I holler out. And sail away.

He hides the sheets somewhere and for a while it seems he has won the Battle of the Bed Sheets until word comes that among

225

Dr. Strother's papers are a number of orders written before he died. One hundred of the sheets are to be cut into bandages and compresses. The other hundred are to be traded for sweet potatoes. The crop is good this year, Dr. Strother noted, and ladies of the area might be only too glad of a chance to trade for a good bed sheet.

Hearing this I think how Dr. Strother's brain worked more in a minute than the Bullfrog's in a year probably.

I cannot respect the Bullfrog. In fact I despise him. For the blood still gushing through him. For the air he swallows. For the liquor he tipples. For the pompous, useless, sermonzing mess of him. Sometimes I squeeze my left hand into a fist and am glad for the growing strength there. Almost enough to choke the life out of his bloated sweaty throat.

Notices, we hear, have gone up in the country stores and village post offices. One is at the dispensary, right by the doorway. *Ladies! Trade Your Bumper Crop of Sweet Potatoes For Fine New Bed Sheets.* On the day appointed, ladies brave the yellow fever scare and arrive in every sort of conveyance. Mule-drawn wagons and buggies, some even on foot, their servants pulling handcarts loaded with sweet potatoes. A few come with children. Most without. They wear fancy clothing and plain faded clothing. Burrell Thomas is in a store-keeper's heaven that will last, we speculate, long as them sheets do.

Guards escort the ladies and their servants to the dispensary where Burrell Thomas apprizes the potatoes, dumping entire bushels out in a heap and making sure all is as fair at the bottom as the top. The ladies apprize the sheets with the same exactitude. Servants or daughters hold the sheet open, the lady walks around it, scrutinizing stitching and hems and material. When she is satisfied as to one side, she has them turn it over and then studies the opposing side in the same way. The sheets look like great blank maps held open in this dull November light. The sheet is carefully folded, then, and the lady leaves without a backward glance at the red-gold heap of potatoes left behind.

I sometimes am able to watch all this from the dispensary window. On the second morning of trading, I see a young woman arrive alone, well toward the end of the line. She is driving two dusty mules and a long wagon. In it are six bushels of sweet potatoes which she begins lifting out herself. Burrell hurries to take over, then gives her two folded sheets. These she don't open. Puts them on the wagon seat, then tries to bargain for more. Burrell begins shaking his head even while she is speaking to him.

I cannot help staring at this one. She is wearing a bright yellow dress and flame-red shawl. Her nose is red from the cold. So are her cheekbones and hands. A dark braid hangs loose from under a hat with a veil flying straight up in the wind. There is nothing special about her in carriage or appearance yet I cannot help staring. Maybe it is the way she hefted out those bushel baskets like a farm hand. Maybe it is because she seems so alone in it all. Alone and wanting all them sheets. I am thinking how Burrell is an ass with those sheets of his. I would have given her a third or even a fourth without dispute.

Plagued with thoughts about that woman. Who she is, where she lives, how far away, and why she needs them sheets. But canvassing serves to take my mind off it for a while.

It is a joke, this canvassing. We ain't free to leave yet can vote in the presidential election. The results, they tell us, will be sent North.

And who do you wish, sir, we ask one

another, playing at fancy-types. Mr. Lincoln or General McClellan?

Both, boys saying. Give 'em each six months and see which of 'em can unsnarl this tangle.

Gives us something to think on. Makes time seem real.

Jewell struts though the wards, engaging anybody who glances his way, anybody stupid enough to listen to him, or anybody who can't do otherwise. I am worried about Marinus even though he is so weak now and does little more than lie on his pallet. Yet if stung hard enough who knows what words he might start spinning off by the yard, besting the man and getting tossed back into the pen, or worse, as his reward.

Jewell is a McClellan-ite and is trying to rally support for the Peace Party. Union and Constitution and States' Rights! he harangues us. Justice, Humanity, Liberty, and the Public Welfare.

Sickening words, in my estimation.

He tells us the current administration is shamefully disregarding our suffering. Tells us if McClellan wins, we will all be set free in no time. We are brave men, he tells us, who deserve better'n martyrdom on account of that Illinois beast, that drunk fool of a mole-eyed monster.

I tell Marinus all this later. Tell him I want to kill the man. He puts a hand on my arm.

But I know, and Marinus probably does too, why I want to kill him. It is because I suspect those words of his might be true. And don't want to believe it.

Victory by the sword, boys, he hollers at us, ain't no true victory whatsoever. You all should know that by now.

Who would think, I tell Marinus, that words can be such a torment.

And the doubts they set loose. I don't tell him about those. How I wonder how it could be — a general, a military man, turning his back on any and all military advantage, giving up all that sacrifice and blood, pulling back armies and talking peace.

Talk!

The rebs will have their own way then. But maybe it will be for the best after all. Then we can settle again, each to his own.

Whoever of us is left alive.

The experiment of war has failed, boys! Look around you! Take a good look at what your drunken despot is doing! Oh the monster'll pay for this, wait'n see.

I suspect Marinus thinks even less of Jewell. He surprises me with a saying. Maggoty man feasting in this death-house, in this country of death.

I am going to kill him, I say again.

No, he says.

No! Why not? You'd kill a poisonous snake, wouldn't you?

Has its uses, he says.

You tell me what use this fellow is.

Misery . . . can be useful.

He's gangrene! I say. He's swamp fever spawned from all the cuts and slashes, from the big cut that is all this.

Marinus opens his eyes and gives me one of his assessing looks.

What? I say. Why you looking at me like that.

Then there is Jewell, nearly upon us.

Ira! Been searching all over God's good earth for you. Lookee. He waves something white. Finally caught up with you — don't know how.

He booms his laugh. Hands me a much-handled letter.

There have been no announcements about the arrival of mail. Nothing to raise hope or fear which I now believe to be the light and dark of the same thing. But here I am, holding a letter. The handwriting not familiar to me.

Then I am shaking and dare not look at the envelope. Do not want to see that it has been broken into, its contents plundered.

231

Good thing you slowed down some, Jewell says. By the way, who'd you gentlemen vote for, if I may ask?

McClellan, Marinus says. And I know it is to get rid of him.

Good for you! How about you, Ira?

I don't answer. There are no words in me.

Ah, that's true love for you! No time for the concerns of us lesser mortals.

He hangs about a while, then waddles away, calling to other patients by their Christian names, asking how each one voted.

She thanks me for my letter. She is terribly sorry about my desperate straits, as she calls it. She forgives me for having led the agents to her father.

Breath spills out of me. Did I do that? Was that part of it too? I try to think back but that time is so far away now. It seems likely. Seems why I must have run.

I see myself, then, behind Mr. Casey's counter, facing the man who came, asking questions.

She tells me that after being apprehended in New York, her father had to suffer the ignominy of a public trial in which he was found guilty of dealing in contraband and sentenced to five years in a Federal penitentiary.

Breath spills away again.

. . . Mother has moved us out of Montrose, because it was too difficult for us there. Now we are planning a further move — to Philadelphia. There I hope to continue my violin studies. By the time you read these words, Ira, we may be settled there. I think of you with great fondness and forgiveness. My father did what he thought was right and so did you. That is all we can do in this world. Act according to our own best judgement. I am wishing you a speedy release. There is talk of it daily in the papers. I have conveyed news of your letter, as you asked, to your dear mother and to Mr. J. L. Casey. Both are in good health. They were joyous to hear that you are alive, and expressed great eagerness to hear from you themselves. They will write, I trust, presently. My dear Ira, I do wish you well now and always and remain your friend, Gabrielle Bonhoffer.

I read this letter over many times. I try to see through the words to her heart. Finally I read the words to Marinus but he is far away somewhere. My story of that time offers nothing in the way of entertainment, does not pull him up by the bootstraps, which in any case he don't have. May as well be talking to myself.

In my own heart, I know. It is a letter of farewell. It is like spring-fed pond water.

Warm on top, cavern-cold a few inches below the surface. She wrote it as a balm for her own heart. Wrote it out of some need to do what we are all taught is the right thing to do. Forgive. Give ourselves up to the godly within it. Even when we can scarce bring ourselves to do so. Wrote it as a way of snipping off some dead segment of time. Then going on.

Marinus swoons to the surface. I bathe his forehead with cool cloths. Tell him I am miserable and fit to be shot. We'll get you fixed up, he says in his dreamy way. I say no, not this time. I am pot and kettle overboard for sure. He tells me to save my strength. Not to fuss over trifles.

I lie down and swath my forehead. It is like some bracing wind.

The the wind dies and I am seeing those green-gold eyes of hers, the bronze color of her face. The heaviness settling over me tells me that despondency has won the day, outflanking me on every side. The pain of it seizes up every joint and is about to shatter every last bone.

She has returned, the woman in the yellow and red. This time the wagon is half-filled with loose potatoes and she is demanding six sheets.

Burrell Thomas stands dumb before this wealth. But then shakes his head. No, not six. He can't give her that many. Besides, he don't want to take her whole supply of potatoes. He brings out two baskets. Fills them himself. Goes into the dispensary and comes out with two sheets, hands them to her. She pulls the rig over into the shadow of the dispensary, follows him back inside. I can see she is a kettle about to boil over, her face all fiery, her black eyebrows near meeting. Meanwhile, the guards stand looking in, observing the entertainment. Paying no mind to the other wagons still hanging back, or anything else.

I slip outside. Eye the woman's mules off to the side, in the shadow of the building. Eye the wagon.

A ward-master is walking toward the dispensary but is still quite a distance away. Outside the guard house, guards sit playing cards in the sunshine. I see all this as I keep sliding closer to that wagon.

It is impossible, but I am doing it. In plain view of anyone who might be watching, I am doing it. Climbing into that wagon bed. Laying myself flat atop the potatoes. Then slowly washing them over me, a few at a time. And sinking in my lumpy sea.

As soon as I have done this crazy-man

thing, I am regretful to the gills. Thinking of Marinus. The Weasel.

Thinking always a plague only now more so. I imagine the ruckus, the guards pulling me out, hedgehog-from-hole. But it is too late to think about climbing back out again. We are moving.

Fifteen

She says something to the mules. The wagon turns to the right, it seems. I am waiting for shouts, horses coming. Maybe gunfire. But the wagon creaks on. I can see a bit of sky. Blue as water.

We turn a couple of times more and finally draw into some dark structure. She is talking to the mules again, unhitching them. My heart is leaping away from all this. Trying to. A mule blows through its nose, sighing as it's led off. I hear the woman coming back to the wagon and brace myself. But she goes away again.

After a long while, I ease myself up. Climb down. Am in some sort of shed. There's a buggy. Some harness. A cold wind gusts through. There's low thunder somewhere. Or else a battle. Crouching down alongside the wagon, I take an inventory. Pen, yes. Letter, yes. I button my jacket. Look at my boots. Tell myself to just go — and be damned one way or another.

Loose tin roofing slaps and bangs. From here I can see part of the house. Its white paint looks to be peeling away. It is a fairly plain house. No grand columns or porticos.

Just a long porch along one side and front. There's some fancy woodwork but not much. Nearby is a vegetable garden. But there's no one I can see in that garden or around the house. And no smoke from the chimneys. The place looks used up and lost. The day is darkening and no light burns in any window.

I ease myself into the main barn, planning to wait for night, or at least until the storm passes.

She turns to look at me and I stand there stunned. She is kneeling before somebody lying in the straw. Her shawl is tossed to one side. She has a lantern.

You hurt? she says.

I shake my head.

Then you can lie down over there. She points. There'll be some food by and by. She turns back to the prone man.

I lie down in the straw of an old box stall across from her. Then I see others in this stall.

Rebels. Some in uniform. Some not. Some bandaged. Others groggy or asleep.

The man across the way starts moaning. Easy enough to think I am back in my ward.

You, she says, standing in front of the stall. If you ain't hurt, give me a hand now.

She tells me she wants a fire built up in

the kitchen stove, water boiled. I'll have to chop some wood. She's low on wood.

She leaves the man and rushes toward the house ahead of me. She points to a stump and axe leaning nearby. I start chopping. Carry small chunks inside. I don't look around. I build a fire in the kitchen stove. Bring a bucket of well water in. Boil some. She scrubs her hands red. Cleanses her instruments. Starts ripping one of Burrell Thomas's sheets into strips. No time to wash these as I'd like, she says.

Help me get 'im in here, she says.

She means the dining room, fitted up as a surgery. I glance further into the house, seeing more rebels lying in the parlor.

What's your name? she says.

With my free hand, I point to my throat. Shake my head.

You can't talk?

I indicate that no, I cannot. It is a kind of truth.

She has Yarmony's deftness and Dr. Strother's profound silence when she works. I am holding a pad saturated with chloroform against the wounded fellow's nose. She is probing a festering arm wound. Right at the elbow. A poor place to be hit. At last she extracts a ball that has torn off a sizeable section of flesh and cartilege. She stares into the wound, looking close. Then cauterizes and bandages. Anybody else might cut, she says. But I loathe cutting though I can do it near well enough. What's the matter with your throat?

I shake my head again.

Let me see.

In an instant she's there, hands probing the larynx region, and I holding my breath.

Don't feel to be nothin' wrong. You got your tongue, don't you?

She pries open my mouth. Inspects it all. It's a terrible thing to think, she says, but I have heard they sometimes cut the tongues out of spies. But it looks like that ain't happened to you yet. Those teeth have taken a beating though. Scurvy?

I nod.

If it's your head, she says, I can't do a thing about heads where there's no wound to see. That's beyond me. I expect you are trying to get home just like the rest of these boys. Well I don't blame you. But you took an awful chance, climbing in that wagon. Could of got us both sent to the Kingdom. It's time to eat now. No rest! You can have something if you want. If not, well — Doneraile's that way. Follow the creek. You might run into some of your cavalry up that way. These boys did. I'm so tired.

Her dress is smudged red. Her eyes don't stay long on any one thing now. I follow her out of the barn. Hesitate.

Everything tells me to run.

But I don't.

In the kitchen she says an old servant sometimes comes by to help her but most everyone has left the area in fear of Sherman. Everybody goes, she says. They all go, soon's they can. She means the wounded rebels. I bring in more kindling and chunks. She starts rinsing some greens from the garden. I see blood from the wounded man run off her hands, over those greens. She pulls pans toward her roughly. Drops things. Is making a terrible racket. There's a mess of unwashed crockery around the sink.

I take her arm. Ease her toward the table. Tell me what to do, I say.

I carry food to those of them that are awake and able to eat. Greens. Mashed sweet potatoes. Molasses. They don't seem to care one way or another who I am, or where I am from. Thank you kindly, a few say.

She is not a doctor but a midwife. Her husband was killed in Tennessee last year. She wants to leave. Go somewhere else. Only, people know about her and are directing wounded boys this way. Deserters. Boys scared to face real doctors, she says. Boys slinking around the outskirts of towns, not wanting to face folks. She gets rid of some and just when she thinks she can leave too, more show up. It has been like this, she says, for months. How far are we from the pen? I ask. Five miles, more, she says. Ideas come and go, flitting through me like swallows. Wait it out here. Somehow save Marinus. Run. Head toward Doneraile and the North.

Her head leans toward the picture book she is looking at. She does this every evening, providing nobody else shows up. It is a book about paintings in Italy. I am here three days now. I have had a bath and she has cleaned up the critters from my hair and nether regions. That first night after supper, I walked out in the rain to a far pasture and nearly kept going. But I chanced to look back at the dusky light in the kitchen window. Now I am thinking how it would be a simple thing to steal one of these boys' side arms. I don't know why I don't do that and just go.

Well, maybe I do. Marinus. And now her, too.

That is the problem with freedom.

I am wondering if there is any such thing as freedom in all this world.

The man with the torn-apart elbow has died. The shock, she thinks. Or else there was something more the matter with him. It has shaken her because she thinks she did it. I tell her no. We buried him, gun and all. I believe I am as crazy as she is.

She is not old but not young neither. She don't seem to care about a thing except these boys, getting them up and away from here.

She says one day she is going to set a match to this place and leave.

Go, she tells me, each evening after we eat and I clean up the kitchen for her. Just go, Ira.

There is a scar-like wedge of lines between her dark eyebrows. Also lines like low waves over her forehead. She means to walk away from here. Free the mules and go. Set her hand to the plow, she says, and not look back. Her favorite picture is called The Sacred and Profane Love. She can stare at it for an hour. More. While the clock ticks and sometimes a fellow moans out something in the parlor.

They can keep coming, she says, but I just won't be here. I have the means, she says, to do it.

Where do you want to go? I say, because I like hearing her voice. It is low and quiet, as when she talked to her mules. I like when she's tired and her eyes aren't skittering everywhere but are quiet too.

I want to go here, she says, and points to that picture she likes above all.

Well, I say. Why don't I go with you?

She pretends not to hear me. Or maybe she don't hear me, inside those colors as she is.

I tell her about Marinus, how I want to get him out somehow.

She believes it is impossible. He being sick on top of everything.

But she is not afraid of the fever, I believe. She is not afraid of anything except staying here forever.

While she looks at her picture, I try to make plans but my brain seems about in the same shape as the rest of me. Shriveled thin. It can only go so far before playing out.

I tell her about Gabrielle, about the drugs, and Mr. Casey, and how I ran. It begins to seem a story from my *Soldier's Book*. Only I can't see any ending to it.

She says Maybe it was not a mistake.

I try to puzzle this out.

We can't always see the design to things, she says.

Is there a design to all this? I say.

She says we don't have the eyes to see.

We are just poor critters despite all our puffery and posturing.

In her bathtub I use a cake of scented soap. Hold it to my nose like a pad of chloroform. I crave that bathtub and that soap. Each morning I wake up and think Tonight I will have another bath. I crave it more than food, which tends to make me a little ill. I have boiled my clothes clean as well. The prison is falling away into some mist. Boys keep coming here. We have plenty of work and it keeps thought away, mostly, too. But when it sneaks past the pickets, I feel something scratching down through the insides of me. A thorny thing. Tells me I have abandoned my friend. To Jewell. To them. Have been disloyal beyond all.

Tonight, in the kitchen, she brushed back my hair and said I should give you a haircut.

Her hand there was something.

When she was through with the haircut, there was the thorny thing again, doing its own work.

So I am not too surprised nor too tragically inclined when I hear the gunshot smattering glass all to bits and know, even in my dream, that it is for real. I was dreaming of shovels, of water seeping up, and somebody calling out my name. I open my eyes and there is

245

the Weasel, standing in the doorway of the bedroom.

Alongside me on the night table is a Kerr revolver. I quick reach for it and there is another shot. I don't feel its fire at first. Put on them boots, Ira, and don't make me mad now.

He leads me bleeding past the woman in the hall. She is dressed — sleeps in her clothes so as to be ready for any emergency. She is hollering at them, saying how I helped her care for CSA boys.

The Weasel smirks. Helped you? he says. I am naked. He won't allow me to put on my clothes. Outside, the day feels like cold water rising all around me. She runs out with a strip of Burrell's sheet. Tries to examine my wrist. Guards keep her back.

I tell myself to look at the light. To the east, rose-pink clouds floating north to south. Against the sky, trees so black and ornate they look like God's own handwriting.

They get me up on a horse and I remember Gus's joke about the sailor who joined to shoot secessionists and not break colts. Hear him laugh, in the telling. Then I just look at the country all around, in the new light.

Sixteen

They have me stand on the stool. I feel the sun on my brow and legs. There is no wind to flap open the fine, deep-red dressing gown I am wearing. As they fix the ends of the rope around my thumbs, I look out at the new boys being told their lesson. I am sorry they have to see this.

They pull the stool away and my arms jerk backward and up with sickening force. The upper part of me drops forward, blood filling my head and pounding there. No way to ease the weight of me for those thumbs, those shoulders. I see the hewn-log steps. Three of them. Weathered and splotched with tobacco stains. Feel one shoulder give, then the other, tearing gently apart like the rhizomes I once pulled up in the woods. Bees sting me everywhere. Hot pokers sinking in. The steps swing forward and back as I kick a little. In the distance I hear the Weasel declaiming. I make a fool of myself crying out but at least do not ask the new boys for help. Do not shame them that way.

Then sink into some peace. Awake to find myself still hanging there. The bees come back. Makes me retch, weep. But each move causes the fibers of me to rip apart even more. I say to Harley Shoot me. Just shoot me. He runs away. Somebody laughs. Then I am on some outcrop of rock, overlooking a river far down. In the distance is a mountain with clouds grown up behind it like white bushes. I step off the edge and go there.

Hood's drawing Sherman out of Georgia and in no time yer gonna lose all yer boys gained over the summer, including Atlanta!

These are the first words I recognize as words. And the first voice. It belongs to the Bullfrog.

Ira, he says, you are a plain fool. I don't know why I am bothering here.

I don't either, I hear myself telling him. But I feel safe now, deep inside that mountain and hiding out from the pulsing storm, the volleys and rumbles and grapeshot.

You boys! he hollers. Busted 'im up all to hell. What good's he gonna do me now?

He fiddles and fusses. I don't know what-all he's doing and don't much care. Just need to sleep some more.

Then hear him saying Looks like I have to take it. What can a man do when it's God's own mess.

Don't be a swoonin' girl there, Ira. Ain't

the end-a creation.

The Bullfrog. I burrow in deeper. Feel the stillness all around me. It is good. But after a time the fire finds me again. Eats in everywhere.

Stop moanin' like some old hound, the Bullfrog is saying. Y'aint buried yet. Take a look at this. Kin you see it? She must be smitten with you, boy! Brought back yer clothes. How d'you like that?

He drops the folded items alongside me. And my boots.

What is her name? I say.

Don't know, the Bullfrog says.

I lapse somewhere else again.

Ira? Ira? *Ira.*

What? I finally swim up to say.

Listen to this. *Arma virumque cano, Trojae qui primus ab oris* — He wrote in phrases, you know. P. V. Maro. Like breaths taken. And why is that *Trojae* first in its phrase? Because it means the city of Troy! Where the fighting started, anyhow. That's why. But why ain't it in the first phrase? you might ask.

Marinus? I say. That he ain't dead surprises me. Or else we both are and have found each other in the afterlife.

A terrible thought.

Because it is the *poet singing* that's first.

The fellow jawing at me is Marinus. I am not dreaming. I try to sit up but fire enters both arms again.

No, he says. That ain't right. First comes the arms. *Arma!* Weapons, batteries, grape-shot. Arms and the man I sing. The second most important place being last. The *cano*. The singing! And the singing of what? Of arms! I ain't surprised, are you?

I believe he must be talking about my arms. Trying to tell me something about them.

Then Jewell's voice. Ira, you are about as much use to me now as a pile of mosquito dung.

I sleep some more.

I take inventory. The right thumb broken, in a splint. The right and left shoulders dislocated. In slings.

My left hand gone.

I cannot believe this. I close my eyes, feel the rope there, the heat of that fire, the pulsing itch of it, open my eyes, see nothing but a swath of bandages at the end of my forearm. Is it there? I say to Marinus. Tell me if it's there, under the bandages. It seems it is. Seems it must be. It hurts.

He takes a shaky breath. Son, he says.

They say that sergeant's ball broke up the bone. He had to cut.

No, I say. He didn't. He wanted to. I am going to kill him.

It is too much to think on. I lay back on the branches. Swoon down underneath the pain. See it shimmering above me. Fish scales catching the light. I wake to retch, seeing the Bullfrog laboring over me, sawing off that hand. And probably drunk.

Mr. Lincoln won in camp and in the nation, we hear. True? In our camp, his amounted to the bigger pile of beans. Rebs down in the mouth so maybe it is true. Who did you vote for, Marinus?

Old mole-eye, he says. I did, too, I tell him. Rebs calling all those who dropped beans onto his pile Lincolnpoops. Nobody dares express any satisfaction in the outcome.

Hood, they say, somewhere in Alabama. We are wondering if he will turn, now that the election is over, and fight Sherman.

Going back into the prison again. Why? Nobody knows. Raids in the area? Maybe. Sherman? It's possible. Exchange, you think? Hoo! You're plain luny to think that. What about sweet potatoes? Suppose we'll see any of them? Don't count on it.

And now rain again and everybody growling about having to move in it.

It takes a full day for wards to be emptied, patients and supplies counted and removed. Again we splash down the road, under heavy guard.

Inside, they feed us one sweet potato each and then we are at leisure to enjoy the fresh air and crowds. The veterans here call us lap dogs and other interesting insults. So we keep to ourselves, yet news of the day still reaches us. Sherman's drive south is the main thing. Sherman heading south while Hood, for some reason, stays north of Decatur, skirmishing and fussing around General Thomas's front.

Don't make sense. Why south? we ask one another. Why don't he turn and beat the daylights out of Hood? Bunch up on him.

We don't know why. Know only that it don't bode anything much for us.

Marinus knows of one war, he says, that went on for twenty-seven years. Another for nearly half a century. And then there was a hundred years one.

Thank you very much, I say.

I ask a new prisoner what Grant has been up to.

Cat at a mousehole, he says.

There is little to occupy us in here but these rumors and nonsense and it is an anguish.

In the pocket of my jacket is the pen Dr. Yarmony gave me. I found it there soon after Jewell gave me the clothing. She sewed the pen in place so it wouldn't fall out. The letter, however, is gone. In the long cold hours I occupy myself with this picture: her sewing in that kitchen of hers. A mess of crockery everywhere, everything at sixes and sevens, and the boys in the parlor wanting this or that too, and she just going on and on, doing. Then falling asleep over that book.

Feel like some ghost, and everybody just accepting the lie of me here.

I stepped over the invisible line back and forth three times, five, six. Was he watching a ways off? Waiting to see if I meant it? Heard small splashing sounds, the guard coming, not so snaky and expert as the other. But it was the same one and now my turn to scare him. There we stood facing one another in a 'simmons grove on a warm afternoon, the woods hollowed out and sun pouring in. I sat down in dry leaves. Make him wait, was my thought. make him just stay there guessing. Not able to get on with his guarding. Not knowing if someone else might be sneaking away. Not able to do a thing but think about what he's going to have to do. Meaning shoot me. Let him think that.

These thoughts came with plenty of disgust at the small thing my life is now. I moved leaves about, chancing to uncover a few 'simmons berries brownish-gold and drying. Ate one. They are small but sweet as figs. I searched for others and found a bunch. The more I ate the more I wanted. On hands and knees I foraged and then he was foraging too. I found another bunch and threw one at him, hitting him. He swung around and threw one at me. I ate it. Long as the berries lasted we had a regular war going. He even stood and shook a tree for more ammunition. But no talking. Not a word.

Wind was swishing away in the high branches and light sliding back and forth over the leaves. I leaned back and dozed. He probably figured I had some trick in mind but I was just tired. When I awoke, the same thoughts started rampaging as they do first thing each morning. What can I do to change all this? There must be something. What? These ain't so much thoughts as a jumble of fear. I just sat there and so did he, my mirror. Sky turned deep red in the west. Black limbs made nice designs against it. Warm air swirled around the two of us. Finally I got up. Seemed no point to anything except just going back. He's still out there, guarding the woods.

Now they are saying Exchange. The real thing.

Three hundred and fifty boys.

Out of thousands.

Who can live with that festering inside you? Only three-fifty.

But we do. Imagining, I suppose, that one of those three-fifty will be — Me, myself and I.

It is a foolish speculation, ain't it? I laugh aloud.

Ward-masters going about their work in here as usual. Each day guards drive Burrell Thomas back down the poor road to the dispensary where he can gather what he needs and come back with it. But the Bullfrog keeps to his tent mostly. When he appears among us, he sways like a tree about to topple. And looks like a man with a busted-up heart.

Well, I don't care a penny about his heart. The sooner it goes, the better.

What does it mean? some of the boys asking. Jewell so down in the mouth. I conclude it means nothing. I am long over looking for details radiant with meaning.

Marinus says the worse possible thing has happened to him. Seems he will live, after all.

Trying to cheer me up.

It is just after roll call and we are ordered to form a line inside the main gate.

The former hospital patients and stewards only.

There is the wildest speculation. Rumors and counter-rumors. A storm of nonsense being bandied.

I sit on the ground waiting for what will be next. Heart flutters and stops. Flutters, stops. Flutters. A divided country. Brain saying *nothing*. Body saying *everything*.

Marinus, I can't help saying. What do you think?

I try not to, he says.

Calvin Forrest says Believe they mean to kill us off, marching us in this damn rain.

We are on the road again. There are the sheds with their branch roofs. Still a fine sight.

We are back and that appears to be what was to happen. Feed us beef and beans. Say it is Thanksgiving.

Seems so.

A rebel chaplain even visits us in the wards. Tells us about the conversion of Saul. Saul devoted his entire life to hunting and slaughtering the Lord's disciples. But one day he had a change of heart. Was struck down from his horse by light and heard the Lord's voice. From that time on he devoted his entire life to the Lord. Only, the disciples were still good and afraid of him, wouldn't touch him with a poker until they were convinced by a man named Barnabas that he was no longer a scourge but a whole new fellow. He was Paul! Man of the Lord! So too might we all become new men if only we recognize the light of the Lord shining for all who have eyes to see.

We laugh at this sermon when the chaplain leaves. He was really spouting on about Sherman, we say. Predicting how he'd be knocked down off his war horse, get blinded by light, and turn reb.

Fine to laugh again.

On a day of no rain and a little weak light, I sit on Jewell's log behind the dispensary, out of the wind. I think of that story. Try to imagine it. Struck down by light, dying, then waking up.

At meetings of the Friends with my mother, I always heard the quiet as a solid block of a thing. Then it would start thrumming and vibrating and when someone suddenly spoke, driven to say something or utter verses from the Bible, or ask that a hymn be sung, that block of quiet would crack in two and it would seem lightning had struck.

I asked my mother if she heard anything in that quiet. She said she did not, only her own thoughts when she couldn't help it. Did she sense anything? I asked.

She said Maybe I have not been brought low enough.

On Jewell's log, in this weak sunlight, I am thinking that maybe He is not on high at all but somewhere low. Not on a throne of tinted clouds but in the deepest darkness. I close my eyes. I have been there and so maybe can slide there again. Lord, I say. *Lord.*

Hear nothing.

Open my eyes. No lightning bolts but light all the same. Stronger now and shattering over the pines.

Nothing happens except clouds come and the light goes.

I close my eyes again. Slide downward to a dark quiet place. The sheen of pain clinging to my arm is almost gone. I see good things in that dark. Not see them so much as feel them. How it was with Marinus close by, just there and not yawping. How it was in that woman's kitchen. How it was eating those greens and mashed sweet potatoes. How it was taking those baths. But then I remember my hand and a sickness comes upon me, and fear, and the pain. I slip off the jacket, bunch it against my face so I can weep in private.

Feel hard things in it. Stones.

Stones, it seems, somewhere in the jacket.

Then Calvin's voice. Shouting. Ira! What you doing back here like the Bullfrog! You know what they're saying? Parole!

Open my eyes. It is Calvin Forrest. Even the top of his head reddening.

Don't drive yourself luny, I say.

Try not thinking that it's so when you see officers coming in with a little table and rolls and saying One well man for every ten sick, up to three-eighty-five. Just try not thinking on it!

I get up. Heart chuffing and fluttering again. The peace broken.

Seventeen

We watch reb officers anchor roll books in the wind. One announces: Anybody whose name is read here today but who can't walk up to the table without assistance tomorrow will be disqualified and another parolee picked instead. That understood?

Spasms of hope plague me. At least half the boys in the ward won't be able to walk. I listen to the names. Hear Marinus's. Do not hear mine.

We are all quiet. Later, Calvin tells me his name was not called either.

I tell Marinus he has to go no matter what.

He ain't talking to me now.

I tell him not to be a fool. I tell him his legs will carry him.

His legs may, but I am worried about his heart. I suspect it is giving on him. He is swelling bad.

He draws a rattly breath, tells me he did not hear my name called.

I say It wasn't. But I went when I had a chance. So he has to now.

He says the matter is closed to discussion.

I say When they call your name tomorrow

and you don't go up there, don't expect me to neither if they call me to substitute.

Yet you want me to go without you.

Ain't the same.

By what reasoning?

No damn reasoning! Why d'you want to stay? You got a real chance now.

Because it is ordained.

No it ain't! They called your name. That's what's ordained.

The battle tires me. I turn to watch two brothers in our ward, Jake and Hank. The older one is trying to help the younger who was called but is so doubled up with scurvy it is doubtful that he can take three steps without help. Tomorrow Jake will have to walk seventeen steps on his own. Up and down they go, Jake stumbling into his brother's arms every fourth step.

The Bullfrog comes through the ward saying that tomorrow he'll make his own announcements as to who will go as helpers.

Stewards or patients? someone asks.

Can't say now, boys. Can't say!

Calvin comes by, wondering if he should chance a bribe.

What d'you have? I ask.

He shows us a gold ring that was in three prisons with him. Would be just like the Bullfrog to take it, he says, then not call me.

I think that sounds about right but I don't say it.

He says he has got to do something or go flunk. He rushes off somewhere. Maybe to Jewell.

I put my hand in my pocket and find the pen, still securely fastened. I see it in the Bullfrog's big hand. It is not a pleasant sight. Hank comes up to me, asks what he can do for his brother. I say You want a miracle and I am the wrong person to ask.

Calvin comes back and says he ain't going to do it. Can't. Don't want to be remembering it that way all the time.

He might sell it, I say.

I'd still be thinking of it otherwise. Besides, Sherman's going to turn yet and beat Hood. You watch. I think Sherman has something else in his brain but don't say it. I do not want anybody feeling any worse than we already do. I see Jake's legs buckling on him. Hank says, Now listen, brother, tomorrow you will walk up there like all the rest. You are going to walk up there and sign that roll.

They are back with their parlor table and their roll books. A hard wind scatters some of their papers. They go on a chase and we don't laugh. Then they start calling names from the first ward.

One by one fellows walk, hobble, limp up to that parlor table and lean forward to sign names, promising not to take up arms for the United States until duly exchanged. They walk, some of them, as if to their own funerals. Some take a lot of time, stopping to clear their eyes or catch their breath or just to rest. This don't bother the rebs. They don't care how long it takes, long as we can maneuver and sign our names. Under the rules, that is all that counts. But when a fellow faints en route, they call a substitute right quick. Each time this happens, I hold my breath. But my name is never called. After ten fellows are called and sign, the surgeon from that ward calls the name of a steward or a patient who is fit enough and that fellow joins the chosen bunch.

Two hours later it is our turn. Again I tell Marinus not to be a fool. He is staring straight up at the pine branches. Hank sits with one arm around his brother. They both stand when Jake's name is called. Hank helps him to the end of the shed, then watches him go on alone. He manages about ten feet, walking almost tiptoe. He is unable to come down on his ankles or to work his knees.

He goes down. Hank steps out. A reb says he can't help. We all wait. Jake tries his best to get up, then just lays there still. The reb calls another name. It is Hank's. Somebody shoves him forward a little but he just goes as far as his brother and helps him back to the ward. Another name then, and that fellow goes up in a hurry. Marinus says Some entertainment.

Then his name.

Marinus, I say. I won't go unless you do.

He don't move.

They call his name again.

He stands. Takes one slow step at a time. The rebs don't glance up until he is right there. I watch Marinus signing something in their book and can only hope it is his name and not some fool saying.

I am an empty bucket until I hear my own name called as a substitute.

Then walking forward, no ground under me and everything but that table and those rebs lost to haze.

I know without having to think it that things can go either way now, good or bad, for I am sunk in it, moving through it, and telling myself just don't fall, just keep going.

Even while I tell myself that we should not sign. Not a one of us. But hold out on them. Make 'em free everybody.

Knowing it would never be.

It is a trouble to hold that pen but I do. Form the letters of my name. Lift my hand

and wind riffles the page over and there are all the blank lines waiting to be filled in. Or not.

Gone are reb officers, table, roll books. Seems a dream. Cloud moves in and stays. Looks like rain again. Those not picked calling us the Sheep. Saying we're just being herded somewhere else is all.

But rebs have given us sheep bars of soap and have sheared the shaggy as well. The word Savannah blows through the wards on its own windstorm.

Ain't no man here wants to go any further south.

By evening, they say, we will know for sure.

So we await that millennium. Calvin tells me he is glad he didn't trade his gold ring for nothing.

Sunset now and no sign of anything but time sliding away. Goats bleating Told you so! Calvin says the Bullfrog didn't pick him because of all that talk about the Elect way back. I tell Calvin I don't believe the man can remember that far back. I nearly can't.

We wait.

Orders. Marching orders! All those that signed be ready to march in one hour.

The goats tell us this is a joke. They are transferring us is all. It cheers Calvin a little.

Marinus leaves the ward and I watch with the greatest curiosity. He is not heading for the latrines but toward the dispensary. The Bullfrog comes up, swaying and stinking but managing to say that even though he, Cyrus Jewell, knew sure as day from night he'd fallen afoul of me, he himself felt quite otherwise about me, and there was something to chew over when I get back. You unnerstan' me, boy? I give you a heap-a credit for runnin'. So you just keep on runnin' now and don't stop 'til you get there. His bloated skin quivers. His face is awry with self-pity and righteousness. And I'm telling you something else now. I'm telling you I had to go and take that hand. You know how the gangrene works, boy. Now get you moving there, 'fore they leave you behind, like me.

I swerve away from him. Marinus is not in the dispensary. Not anywhere near it.

I slip into the woods. My only advantage is that I can go a little faster than him. Maybe. I don't call his name. Hearing it, he might just hide on me.

What I know now is that he has tricked me into signing. He did not do it for himself but me.

The woods are quiet with fog and coming night. I have to go slower. Try to look everywhere. There are places to hole up, in thickets and clumps, but I suspect that is not what he is after. I suspect I know what he is after and I am shivering inside with it.

I see him. Or else it is a guard. The figure walks poorly, stopping every so often. I do not call out.

I lose track of direction, fear getting lost. He is not on a straight course but swerving and cutting back as if looking for some trail. I pass a large pine, one of the marker trees. Just get a glimpse of that white X. What's worse is that my strength is playing out on me.

I am as mad at the fellow as ever I was.

Then I don't see him anymore. I stop. Turn back, go a few steps when I hear the word *son* spoken right close by.

Turns my blood the other way, leaving me dizzy.

He's sitting against a pine. Head back. Eyes closed.

What did you go and do, Marinus? I whisper. Let's get back. Quick.

This is better — For me.

Listen, I say. We'll stick. We'll be together. Even after if you want. This ain't the time to sink, to give up.

It is raying through me. That I can get him well and then we'll — I see no one thing but many things, a blur of them.

Ira, he says. You go — Live.

I am working at pulling him up when we hear the music. Harmonica music. A slow waltz. It's that guard.

We got mixed up in the woods, I tell him when he gets up close and sees us. We're going back right now. We been paroled.

He has his carbine in right hand, harmonica in left.

Friend, he says, yer lyin' to me.

No I ain't.

Run twice, I git to shoot you. That's the rule. Fair and square.

Marinus says, in his old voice, Then you'll have to shoot me as well.

The guard says he can do that all right. But we can try runnin' if we want. He'll give us a start. Might be agreeable, in the dark.

Marinus says to let me go. Take him instead. Here, he says. I have something you might be interested in.

The guard says he can't do it that way. But he is curious to see what Marinus has squirreled away there. I am too. Marinus brings out his hand, closed around something. Extends it. The guard leans in too close and Marinus heaves himself at the fellow's knees. The guard pitches over atop him. They scrabble but Marinus is no match for the fellow. I go after that carbine. Swing it, catching the guard on the head. Swing again. It wrenches me apart again but I keep at it, not able to stop.

Marinus is down and not breathing. I lean over him, wait a long time but there is no sign. Nothing. Then I start hearing things. Son, I hear. Do what you are afraid of doing, always.

But it seems I am afraid of everything equally right now. I sit and listen to rain plinking down on the leaves. Then hear a scratching and scrabbling.

Chipmunk. Still foraging.

Nothing on the ground of any treasure. Only the shiny harmonica. Feels warm. I put it on the fellow's chest. He is young. Without that hat on, he looks real young.

I go back to Marinus. Know that he is gone. For good this time, it seems. But I stay alongside him anyway, hand on his forehead. I keep whispering his name.

He has fooled me before.

Eighteen

I mean to go back. It's what I fear the most. Go back and tell Burrell Thomas, then slip in with the boys who are to go, if it ain't too late.

And if it is?

Don't know. Ain't thinking much about it. Just moving. If another guard finds me, another guard finds me. But it is getting on dark now so I might be lucky.

Nothing looks familiar. No tree. No rock outcrop. No dip or rise in the land. I come to no big pines with those white X's. When it is too dark to see anything much, I know I am lost.

In every which way.

In a hollow I lay in leaves, cover myself with them. Tuck myself away under the jacket. Let the pain have its way.

If there is any thought, it is this: another snag of sticks broken and the river taking me somewhere else.

Sleep a blessed thing.

I come back into myself slowly. The pain is there waiting for me, and the knowing.

Marinus gone. And that guard, maybe. And my hand. I have no more desire to kill anything. Not even the Bullfrog. A bird somewhere chirps. Sounds clean as a bright color. Yellow.

Sunlight rays through a ground fog. The earth smells of wet leaves. Moss. Lichens. Woodrot. It is so peaceful I cannot believe I am still among the living. I lie here wrapped in a kind of peaceful pain. One side of my face against acorns, maybe. Or stones. I investigate.

It is a small string of pearls. In the lining of the jacket. Also find greenbacks enough to take me all the way North.

I sit looking at this bounty, belly churning.

Sometimes you know a thing so clearly you do not even have to know. And it is the purest sort of thing.

I creep downhill. Every twig snapped sets off a clanging. I stop then and wait for the quiet to settle in. Start creeping again. Tree to tree. Mossy rock to rock. There are some nice long stretches of pine needles and I glide over these hawk-fashion, down, down, down.

Hear it before I see it. Smell it.

A stream.

Drink long and hard.

Take bearings from the sun. Walk in the sound of that water. Stone to flat slippery stone.

And there is a town.

So-called civilization, I hear Marinus saying.

He winks at me a little. I mash mud across my face. With my bandages and in my gray outfit, I am any reb.

Doneraile.

I slide out of that town again. Slink down to that stream.

Flow south with it.

Where, you might say, I least want to go.

At a farm I stop to ask. Make my voice a reb voice. The Negro woman points. Tells me to wait. Comes back with a wedge of apple pie. Tin cup of milk.

I glide southward, belly full of food, body full of fire, and brain starting up its own rebellion.

What kind of way is this to be a footprint?

It is no surprise to me, the lost feeling of her place. Reminds me of Marinus himself. You take the spirit out of a thing and it is dead. It is a husk waiting for winter to trample it into the earth.

In the shed is the wagon. I do not see the mules. The garden is dug up more. In the first pasture there's the grave we made for that fellow.

Only one boy in the barn, in the box stall.

She here? I say in my reb voice.

Was, he says.

When?

Oh —

And that's all he says. Has a stone jug alongside him. Shadows crisscross my heart. His leg is bandaged at the knee. Bandages don't look newly changed.

I sit with him a while but he seems disinclined toward talk. Stupefied is the word.

I creep across the yard to the house. No one in the kitchen. The stove cold, a clutter of plates and what-not around the sink. No one in the parlor, the front hall. Steps creak under me and I am the ghost. A cold wind blows in through the shot-out window in the bedroom that was mine. The bed looks about as I left it. The Kerr revolver is gone. I close the door and open the one across the hall.

Her room, too, is empty. No evidence of the yellow dress. The red shawl. The black hat. I think how she said she was going to take a match to it all.

Gives me hope.

I am on a ship called *The Star of the South*. Marinus and I are washing with great bars of soap while a sailor holds our belongings high up out of danger from the shenanigans of the others splashing water at one another. Our belongings consist of Marinus's book and my pen. My clothing floats away on gray waves. The boots have sunk almost right away. We can hear music, a quadrille being played somewhere in the ship. Can smell coffee brewing. They have new uniforms for us, they tell us. No one will look at us directly. They look off to the side or somewhere above our heads. Don't want to see all the bones. I am astonished by so much space all around us. Ocean to one side, a haze of smoky blue-gray to the other, and the bloody sun floating down into it. It is pleasant seeing the dead line so far off in the distance. Rising and tilting and falling with the ship but so far away it seems to have nothing to do with us whatsoever.

Whales appear. And their calves. The calves weave in and out of the plane of water as if sewing together sky and sea.

Bliss and light slide over me like waves. I rock in their trough. Their colors. Green and blue and silver and I am one of those whales streaming with light.

It is a quilt, those colors. A quilt over me as I lie on the settee in the parlor.

They'll be back for you, she is saying. Haul you away again. Maybe worse.

She is in the doorway.

No words come to any rescue. I almost do not recognize her because she is not wearing the yellow dress but something heavier and dark and seems an apparition. Or part of my dream.

Had only one left, she is saying. But knew better than to hope. She unties her hat. Throws it onto a chair. There's coffee, she says.

Turns toward the kitchen.

I moan, trying to get up.

You hurt? she says, her back to me.

No, I say.

She turns to me. Sees my arm. Sees me holding onto the shoulder. Sees the glazing of sweat, probably, and paleness of nausea.

Come into the surgery.

Dining room, she means.

It is hard to believe, I say. But I am a free man.

She takes these words in without a word.

Then I remember what I have come to say. How I did not want to take her means.

She says Well I wanted somebody to have some use of it.

Then gets down to work. Plunking shoulder back into place. Resetting and splinting the thumb. Cleansing the stump that is worse, to my eye, than anything in dream.

The house is quiet around us. I think this is what she wanted to run from — that quiet.

She looks at me. Breaks that thrumming all around us. I have forgotten your name, she says.

Ira, I say.

Three more boys arrive and we are working too hard for any other sort of talk.

We squabble, from time to time, almost as bad as Marinus and I did. I get in her way or do things wrong, or she won't take a good long rest, or she wants me to go North, get away, orders me to, says I'll die here sure as anything, and I say I'd like to go but can't, too much to do around this damn place. I tell her she just wants to be a crazy martyr and she tells me about the same and we sulk a little when the shot hits in too deep, and maybe feel sorry for ourselves. But despite it all, I recognize the symptoms and they scare me half witless, but there it is. The shakiness and flare of heat when she gets too close, or in the kitchen when I am washing up things and she is at the table with that blasted book and drowsing over it and I know will want to go upstairs soon, and I have the water all ready for a good long hot bath for her and so am jittery as right before the Wilderness, and yes, wanting to run, too, run away, save myself, scared of everything, scared I won't be man enough when the time comes, or she won't let the time come, will just push it aside, push me aside, rough as ever Louie was, or worst of all will feel sorry for me and will brush back my hair or some such idiotic thing and say Thank you, Jacob, you are very kind and a great help but I am an old woman and it won't do at all, you know, and besides they'll be here looking for you, will kill you this time, and so I want you to go.

Jacob. The name she has given me in case boys spread word of me in these parts.

As if a name will help!

Fear seeps like a bruise over me and all through me, but stronger than fear is the knowing that I have come this far and maybe there is some design to it after all, who knows? a design that might take me there, I just have to do this now, and believe, do this now and be ready, be enough, in my heart, enough for her and for the whole of it, even the fear, wait and will the whole as ever Gus willed Grant to win for the good of the Union.

Her name is Anna Marie Donnelly.

Don't dare say her Christian name aloud yet but one day will. As I say it now, to myself.

Anna Marie.

As I put my hand on the small bones of her shoulder and say It's time.

I'll stand watch while you sleep, I tell her. I'll take care of any boys who come unless its real bad, then I'll wake you. This I promise so she'll sleep easy, sleep deep.

And I'll keep water hot on the stove, and Burrell's bandages ready, and food or whiskey, if they need whiskey to get themselves through, and if it's the Weasel who comes, well I have the revolver and will use it and will bury the man deep and won't omit a prayer.

But for now I lean over her, smell that cake of soap she must use on her hair.

Time for a bath and a good long rest, I say. I'll get the water up.

Well past midnight. A December night, stars touching the hill of pasture, the curve there, like the sea. And we riding it somewhere under the threads of light, all a tangle, all a maze. A prayer, then, for my dead. For Gus and Willy and Louie, too, in case he died or even if he didn't, and for my father and grandfather and Dr. Strother, and for Marinus, who somehow needed to die. Maybe one day I will know the reason, if even there is one. And for that dead guard, if he died, and the one in the pile so long ago, and boys in battlefield graves, and for the ones in the muck and cold of prison camps, and in fields and in the black of woods, and boys in training camps and on marches and on the sea and on the rivers of this land and in hospitals everywhere, and for these boys here and for her.

It is not so much a praying as a holding of it all in some center of me, and it raying out to those very stars like some small answering signal across so much dark.

Hardly reasonable, under the circumstances. But what is reasonable? Is rain? Is wind? Are waves? Trees? These stars? What is reasonable? — something we just make up. What is hope or courage or love? Something we are. This is all I can lay claim to in the way of knowing anything now. Maybe it is nothing or next to nothing, yet seems to fill the amplitude I am tonight. I am this night, this dark, I am this peace and this war, I am courage and fear, hope and despair, hate and forgiveness, I am hell and I am heaven, there is no end to me, nor to what I can do, it seems, tonight. A good joke, for I know what I am. A few sticks of bones held in this meager and frayed pouch of flesh. But how these bones burn, the best kindling!

Acknowledgements

Although the novel's major characters are fictional, several minor characters as well as many events depicted within it are drawn from an account "prepared from" the daily journal of Robert H. Kellogg, Sergeant-Major, 16th Regiment, Connecticut Volunteers, and an exchanged prisoner of war. The edited account was published by L. Stebbins of Hartford, Connecticut, in 1865, a few months before the end of the Civil War. That this account was hurried into print and intended to move Northern generals and politicians to press for a prisoner-of-war agreement seems evident, given the book's title, subtitle, and epigraph. *Life and Death in Rebel Prisons: Giving A Complete History of the Inhuman (sic) and Barbarous Treatment of Our Brave Soldiers by Rebel Authorities, Inflicting Terrible Suffering and Frightful Mortality, Principally at Andersonville, Ga., and Florence, S.C., . . . To Which Is Added As Full Sketches Of Other Prisons As Can Be Given Without Repetition of the above, by Parties Who Have Been Confined Therein.* "We speak that we do know, and testify that we have seen."

I've also drawn liberally from a pocket-sized handbook printed in 1862 in Cambridge, Massachusetts, by H. O. Houghton, entitled *Soldier's Diary, and Book for Leisure Moments*, compiled by the Massachusetts Sabbath School Society and intended for distribution to the young Christian soldier going forth "in defence of his country." Lined pages for each month of the year alternate with a "Golden Treasury" of counsel and hints for the well-being of body and spirit. The copy which I found in an antiquarian bookshop in Sayre, Pennsylvania — not far from Elmira, New York, site of one of the most notorious Northern prisons for captured Confederate soldiers — has no events or thoughts recorded on its brown-spattered, lined journal pages. Someone — perhaps a child or perhaps even a prisoner — has pencilled in a few numerals in imitation of those meant to represent the days of the month for January.

Other sources for this novel include several of the major historical texts on the Civil War, including General Ulysses S. Grant's *Personal Memoirs* (reprinted by the AMS Press in New York, in 1972, from the 1894 edition published in New York by Charles L. Webster and Company) and *Harper's Pictorial History of The Civil War*, by Alfred H. Guernsey and Henry M. Alden, cited in the

Foreword. *The Andersonville Diary and Memoirs of Charles Hopkins* (edited by William B. Styple and John J. Fitzpatrick and published in Kearney, New Jersey by the Belle Grove Publishing Company, 1988) proved very helpful for details of place as well as for the hanging incident.

Also of great help: Stewart Brooks' *Civil War Medicine*, published by Charles C. Thomas in Springfield, Illinois, 1966. Arnold and Connie Krochmal's *A Guide to the Medicinal Plants of the United States*, published by The New York Times Book Company in 1973. And *Images of Healing*, edited by Ann Novotny and Carter Smith, with an Introduction by William D. Sharpe, M.D., published in New York by the Macmillan Publishing Company, Inc., 1980.

Finally I must acknowledge "Sumner's Resolutions on the Theory of Secession and Reconstruction," February 11, 1862, reprinted in *Documents of American History*, edited by Henry Steele Commager and published in New York by Appleton-Century-Crofts, 1968.

Captain Wirz, the commander at Andersonville, is a historical person, as is Lieutenant Davis. The doctors Yarmony and Strother are historical persons though I've taken liberties with their appearance; Dr.

283

Strother did come down with yellow fever but in fact survived, according to *Life and Death In Rebel Prisons*, cited above.

I'm deeply grateful to my husband Jerry for his infinite patience and encouragement and for inspiring the final version of this work. And to Virginia Sheret, my other excellent first reader, for her perceptive comments and sustaining enthusiasm. Many thanks, as well, to Jack Vernon for offering an invaluable suggestion regarding nineteenth century colloquial expression, and to Pat Roberts, Erich Hooper, and Douglas Hooper for their help at various stages of the work.

Valerie Holmes-Shook and Betty Smith of the Susquehanna County Historical Society and Free Library Association in Montrose, Pennsylvania, provided copies of Civil War letters and actual Montrose newspapers from the 1860's; my great thanks to them and to the Historical Society for its fine Civil War-era display and collection.

A grant from the Pennsylvania Council on the Arts allowed me to spend a year researching the life of General Grant — work leading indirectly to this novel. A Fellowship in Creative Writing from the National Endowment for the Arts in 1989 afforded me the time and resources to work on this project, among others. To both of these fine organizations, my warm gratitude.